"It's ob_____n us...."

Having _____ be the worst idea ever.

They were polar opposites. He was wild and exciting and Gracie wasn't. At least, she was doing her damndest to prove that she wasn't.

And that was the problem in a nutshell. Jesse called to the bad girl inside of her.

Not happening. She had an image to uphold. A reputation to protect. She was town mayor, for heaven's sake.

Anxiety rushed through her, because as committed as she was to the path she'd chosen, she couldn't help but feel as if she'd missed out on something.

She wanted one more night with Jesse. One more memory. Then she could stop fantasizing and go back to her nice, conservative life and step up as the town's new mayor without any worries or regrets.

She *would*. But not just yet.

She slammed on the brakes, swung the car around and headed for the motel.

"Okay," she blurted ten minutes later when Jesse opene_____s do it."

Dear Reader,

What do you get when you combine one wild, wicked, dangerously handsome cowboy, a botched bank heist and a truckload of premium grade-A moonshine? The first book in my new The Texas Outlaws trilogy, featuring the hot, hunky Chisholm brothers.

Three-time pro bull rider Jesse James Chisholm is desperate to forget his past—particularly the sins of his outlaw father—and get the hell out of Lost Gun, Texas. The only trouble? He isn't all that anxious to leave the girl who once stole his heart.

Soon-to-be mayor Gracie Stone wants nothing more than to see her old flame leave Lost Gun and never look back. Maybe then she can forget Jesse's touch and his kiss and...oh, boy. Gracie has a town to run and she certainly doesn't need the resident bad boy tarnishing her good-girl reputation.

But Gracie isn't half the good girl she pretends to be. Even more, she can't seem to keep her distance when it comes to Jesse. Likewise, Jesse is having trouble keeping his boots on and his hands off where Gracie is concerned.

I hope you enjoy reading Jesse and Gracie's story as much as I enjoyed writing it! I would love to hear from you. You can visit me online at www.kimberlyraye.com or friend me on Facebook.

Much love from deep in the heart...

Kimberly Raye

Texas Outlaws: Jesse

—

Kimberly Raye

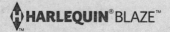

Recycling programs
for this product may
not exist in your area.

ISBN-13: 978-0-373-79784-4

TEXAS OUTLAWS: JESSE

Copyright © 2014 by Kimberly Groff

Printed in U.S.A.

HARLEQUIN®
www.Harlequin.com

ABOUT THE AUTHOR

USA TODAY bestselling author Kimberly Raye started her first novel in high school and has been writing ever since. To date, she's published more than fifty novels, two of them prestigious RITA® Award nominees. She's also been nominated by *RT Book Reviews* for several Reviewer's Choice awards, as well as a career achievement award. Currently she is writing a romantic vampire mystery series for Ballantine Books that is in development with ABC for a television pilot. She also writes steamy contemporary reads for Harlequin's Blaze line. Kim lives deep in the heart of the Texas Hill Country with her very own cowboy, Curt, and their young children. She's an avid reader who loves Diet Dr. Pepper, chocolate, Toby Keith, chocolate, alpha males (*especially* vampires) and chocolate. Kim also loves to hear from readers. You can visit her online at www.kimberlyraye.com.

Books by Kimberly Raye

HARLEQUIN BLAZE

To get the inside scoop on Harlequin Blaze and its talented writers, be sure to check out blazeauthors.com.

This book is dedicated to Curt,
My loving husband and best friend,
You still know how to rock a pair of Wranglers!

1

THIS WAS TURNING into *the* worst ride of his life.

Jesse James Chisholm stared over the back of the meanest bull this side of the Rio Grande at the woman who parked herself just outside the railing of the Lost Gun Training Facility, located on a premium stretch of land a few miles outside the city limits.

His heart stalled and his hand slipped. The bull lurched and he nearly tumbled to the side.

No way was *she* here.

No frickin' *way*.

The bull twisted and Pro Bull Riding's newest champion wrenched to the right. He was seeing things. That had to be it. He'd hit the ground too many times going after that first buckle and now it was coming back to haunt him. His grip tightened and his breath caught. Just a few more seconds.

One thousand three. One thousand four.

"Jesse!" Her voice rang out, filling his ears with the undeniable truth that she was here, all right.

Shit.

The bull jerked and Jesse pitched forward. He flipped and went down. Hard.

Dust filled his mouth and pain gripped every nerve in his already aching body. The buzzer sounded and voices echoed, but he was too fixated on catching his breath to notice the chaos that suddenly surrounded him. He shut his eyes as his heart pounded in his rib cage.

Come on, buddy. You got this. Just breathe.

In and out. In. Out. In—

"Jesse? Ohmigod! Are you all right? Is he all right?"

Her desperate voice slid into his ears and stalled his heart. His eyes snapped open and sure enough, he found himself staring into a gaze as pale and blue as a clear Texas sky at high noon.

And just as scorching.

Heat swamped him and for a split second, he found himself sucked back to the past, to those long, endless days at Lost Gun High School.

He'd been at the bottom of the food chain back then, the son of the town's most notorious criminal, and no one had ever let him forget it. The teachers had stared at him with pity-filled gazes. The other boys had treated him like a leper. And the girls… They'd looked at him as if he were a bona fide rock star. The bad boy who was going to save them from the monotony of their map-dot existence.

Every girl, that is, except for Gracie Stone.

She'd been a rock star in her own right. Buck wild and reckless. Constantly defying her strict adoptive parents and pushing them to the limits. They'd wanted a goody-goody daughter befitting the town's mayor and first lady, and Gracie had wanted to break out of the neat little box she'd been forced into after the tragic death of her real parents.

They'd both been seniors when they'd crossed paths at a party. It had been lust at first sight. They'd had three scorching weeks together before they'd graduated and she'd ditched him via voice mail.

We just don't belong together.

For all her wicked ways, she was still the mayor's daughter, and he was the son of the town's most hated man. Water and oil. And everyone knew the two didn't mix.

Not then, and certainly not now.

He tried to remember that all-important fact as he focused on the sweet-smelling woman leaning over him.

She looked so different compared to the wild and wicked girl who lived and breathed in his memories. She'd traded in too much makeup and too little clothes for a more conservative look. She wore a navy skirt and a white silk shell tucked in at the waist. Her long blond hair had been pulled back into a no-nonsense ponytail. Long thick lashes fringed her pale blue eyes. Her lips were full and pink and luscious.

Different, yet his gut ached just the same.

He stiffened and his mouth pressed into a tight line. "Civilians aren't allowed in the arena." He pushed himself to his feet, desperate to ignore the soft pink-tipped fingers on his arm. "Not without boots." Her touch burned through the material of his Western shirt and sent a fizzle of electricity up his arm. "And jeans," he blurted. "And a long-sleeve shirt, for Chrissake." Damn, but why did she have to keep touching him like that? "You're breaking about a dozen different rules."

"I'm sorry. You just hit the ground so hard and I thought you were hurt and..." Her words trailed off and she let her hand fall away.

He ignored the whisper of disappointment and concentrated on the anger roiling inside him. "You almost got me killed." That was what he said. But the only thing rolling over and over in his mind was that she'd put herself in danger by climbing over the railing with a mean sumbitch bull on the loose.

He pushed away the last thought because no way— no friggin' way—did Jesse care one way or the other when it came to Gracie Stone. He was over her.

Finished.

Done.

He held tight to the notion and focused on the fact that she'd ruined a perfectly good training session. "You don't yell at a man when he's in the middle of a ride. It's distracting. I damn near broke my neck." He dusted off his pants and reached for his hat a few feet away. "If you're looking for City Hall—" he shook off the dirt and parked the worn Stetson on top of his head "—I think you're way off the mark."

"Actually, I was looking for you." Unease flitted across her face as if she wasn't half as sure of herself as she pretended to be. She licked her pink lips and he tried not to follow the motion with his eyes. "I need to talk to you."

He had half a mind to tell her to kick her stilettos into high gear and start walking. He was smack-dab in the middle of a demonstration for a prospective buyer who'd flown in yesterday to purchase the black bull currently snorting in a nearby holding pen.

Because Jesse was selling his livestock and moving on.

Finally.

With the winnings and endorsements from his first championship last year, he'd been able to put in an offer for a three-hundred-acre spread just outside of Austin, complete with a top-notch practice arena. The seller had accepted and now it was just a matter of signing the papers and transferring the money.

"Yo, Jesse." David Burns, the buyer interested in his stock, signaled him from the sidelines and Jesse held up a hand that said hold up a minute.

David wanted to make a deal and Jesse needed to get a move on. He didn't have time for a woman who'd ditched him twelve years ago without so much as a face-to-face.

At the same time, he couldn't help but wonder what could be so almighty important that it had Lost Gun's newly elected mayor slumming it a full ten miles outside the city limits.

He shrugged. "So talk."

Her gaze shifted from the buyer to the group of cowboys working the saddle broncs in the next arena. Several of the men had shifted their attention to the duo standing center stage. "Maybe we could go someplace private."

The words stirred all sorts of possibilities, all treacherous to his peace of mind since they involved a very naked Gracie and a sizable hard-on. But Jesse had never been one to back down from a dangerous situation.

He summoned his infamous slide-off-your-panties drawl that had earned him the coveted title of Rodeo's

Hottest Bachelor and an extra twenty thousand fol-
lowers on Twitter and eyed her. "Sugar, the only place
I'm going after this is straight into a hot shower." He
gave her a sly grin he wasn't feeling at the moment
and winked. "If you're inclined to follow, then by all
means, let's go."

Her eyes darkened and for a crazy instant, he
glimpsed the old Gracie. The wild free spirit who'd
stripped off her clothes and gone skinny-dipping with
him their first night together.

But then the air seemed to chill and her gaze narrowed. "We'll talk here," she said, her voice calm and
controlled. A total contradiction to the slight tremble of
her bottom lip. She drew a deep breath that lifted her
ample chest and wreaked havoc with his self-control. "A
fax came in from the production company that filmed
Famous Texas Outlaws."

The mention of the television documentary that had
nearly cost him his livelihood all those years ago was
like a douse of ice water. "And?"

"They sold rights to a major affiliate who plans to
air the show again and film a live 'Where Are They
Now?' segment. They're already running promos for
it. Sheriff Hooker had to chase two fortune hunters off
your place just yesterday."

His "place" amounted to the burned-down shack
and ten overgrown acres on the south end of town that
he'd once shared with his father and brothers. As for
the fortune hunters, well, they were out of luck. There
was nothing to find.

His lawyer had been advising him to sell the property for years now, but Jesse had too many bad mem-

ories to want to profit off that sad, miserable place. Ignoring it had been better. Easier.

He eyed her. "When?"

"It's airing next Tuesday." She squared her shoulders, as if trying to gather her courage. "I thought you deserved fair warning after what happened the last time."

His leg throbbed at the memory. "So that's why you're here?" He tamped down the sudden ache. "To give me a heads-up?"

She nodded and something softened inside him.

A crazy reaction since he knew that her sudden visit had nothing to do with any sense of loyalty to him. This was all about the town. She'd traded in her wild and wicked ways to become a model public servant like her uncle. Conservative. Responsible. Loyal.

He knew that, yet the knotted fist in his chest eased just a little anyway.

"I know you just got back yesterday," she went on, "but I really think it would be better to cut your visit short until it's all said and done." She pulled her shoulders back. The motion pressed her delicious breasts against the soft fabric of her blouse. He caught a glimpse of lace beneath the thin material and he knew then that she wasn't as conservative as she wanted everyone to think. "That would make things a lot easier."

"For me?" He eyed her. "Or for you?"

Her gaze narrowed. "I'm not the one they'll be after."

"No, you're just in charge of the town they'll be invading. After all the craziness the last time I think you're anxious to avoid another circus. Getting rid of me would certainly help." The words came out edged with challenge, as if he dared her to dispute them.

He did.

She caught her bottom lip as if she wanted to argue, but then her mouth pulled tight. "If the only eyewitness to the fire is MIA, the reporters won't have a reason to stick around. I really think it would be best for everyone." Her gaze caught and held his. "Especially you."

Ditto.

He sure as hell wasn't up to the pain he'd gone through the first time. The show had originally aired a few months after he'd graduated high school, five years to the day of his father's death. He'd been eighteen at the time and a damn sight more reckless.

He'd been ground zero in the middle of a training session with a young, jittery bull named Diamond Dust. A group of reporters had shown up, cameras blazing, and Diamond had gone berserk. More so than usual for a mean-as-all-get-out bucking bull. Jesse had hit the ground, and then the bull had hit him. Over and over, stomping and crushing until Jesse had suffered five broken ribs, a broken leg, a dislocated shoulder and a major concussion. Injuries that had landed him in a rehab facility for six months and nearly cost him everything.

Not that the same thing wouldn't have happened eventually. He'd been on a fast road to trouble back then, ignoring the rules and riding careless and loose. The reporters had simply sped up the inevitable, because Jesse hadn't been interested in a career back then so much as an escape.

From the guilt of watching his own father die and not doing a damned thing to stop it.

It wasn't your fault. The man made his own choice.

That was what Pete Gunner had told him time and time again after the fire. Pete was the pro bull rider who'd taken in thirteen-year-old Jesse and his brothers and saved them from being split up into different foster homes after their father had died. Pete had been little more than a kid himself back then—barely twenty— and had just won his first PBR title. The last thing he'd needed was the weight of three orphans distracting him from his career, but he'd taken on the responsibility anyway. The man had been orphaned himself as a kid and so he'd known how hard it was to make it in the world. Cowboying had saved him and so he'd taught Jesse and his brothers how to rope and ride and hold their own in a rodeo arena. He'd turned them into tough cowboys. The best in the state, as a matter of fact. Even more, he'd given them a roof over their heads and food in their stomachs, and hope.

And when Diamond had nearly killed Jesse, it had been Pete who'd paid for the best orthopedic surgeons in the state. Pete was family—as much a brother to Jesse as Billy and Cole—and he was about to marry the woman of his dreams this Saturday.

That was the real reason Jesse had come back to this godforsaken town. And the reason he had no intention of leaving until the vows were spoken, the cake was cut and the happy couple left for two weeks in the Australian outback.

Then Jesse would pack up what little he had left here and head for Austin to make a real life. Far away from the memories. From her.

He stiffened against a sudden wiggle of regret.

"Trust me, there's nothing I'd like better than to haul ass out of here right now."

"Good. Then we're on the same page—"

"But I won't," he cut in. "I can't."

A knowing light gleamed in her eyes. "I'm sure Pete would understand."

"I'm sure he would, but that's beside the point." Jesse shook his head. "I'm not missing his wedding."

"But—"

"You'll just have to figure out some other way to defuse the situation and keep the peace."

And then he did what she'd done to him on that one night forever burned into his memory—he turned and walked away without so much as a goodbye.

2

WAIT A SECOND.

Wait just a friggin' *second.*

That was what Gracie wanted to say. She'd envisioned this meeting about a zillion times on the way over, and this wasn't the way it had played out. Where was the gratitude? The appreciation? The desperate embrace followed by one whopper of a kiss?

She ditched the last thought and focused on the righteous indignation that came with violating about ten different city ordinances on someone else's behalf. Leaking private city business to civilians was an unforgivable sin and the memo from the production company had been marked strictly confidential.

But this was Jesse, and while she'd made it a point to avoid him for the past twelve years, she couldn't in good conscience sit idly by and let him be broadsided by the news crew currently on its way to Lost Gun.

Not because she cared about him.

Lust. That was all she'd ever felt for him. The breath-stealing, bone-melting, desperate lust of a hormone-driven sixteen-year-old. A girl who'd dreamed of a world beyond her desperately small town, a world filled with bright lights and big cities and a career in photojournalism.

She'd wanted out so bad back then. To the point that she'd been wild and reckless, eager to fill the humdrum days until her eighteenth birthday with whatever excitement she could find.

But then she'd received the special-delivery letter announcing that her older brother had been killed in the line of duty and she'd realized it was time to grow up, step up and start playing it safe right here in Lost Gun.

For her sister.

Charlotte Stone was ten years younger than Gracie. And while she'd been too young—four years old, to be exact—to remember the devastation when their parents had died in a tragic car accident, she'd been plenty old enough at nine to feel the earthquake caused by the death of their older brother. She'd morphed from a happy, outgoing little girl, into a needy, scared introvert who'd been terrified to let her older sister out of her sight.

Gracie had known then that she could never leave Lost Gun. Even more, she'd vowed not only to stay but to settle down, play it safe and make a real home for her sister.

She'd traded her beloved photography lessons for finance classes at the local junior college and ditched everything that was counterproductive to her new safe, settled life—from her favorite fat-filled French fries to Jesse Chisholm himself.

Especially Jesse.

He swiped a hand across his backside to dust off his jeans and her gaze snagged on the push-pull of soft faded denim. Her nerves started to hum and the air stalled in her lungs.

While time usually whittled away at people, making them worn around the edges, it had done the opposite with Jesse. The years had carved out thick muscles and a ripped bod. He looked even harder than she remembered, taller and more commanding. The fitted black-and-gray retro Western shirt framed broad shoulders and a narrow waist. Worn jeans topped with dusty brown leather chaps clung to trim hips and thighs and stretched the length of his long legs. Scuffed brown cowboy boots, the tips worn from one too many run-ins with a bull, completed the look of rodeo's hottest hunk. The title had been held by local legend Pete Gunner up until he'd proposed to the love of his life just two short years ago. Since then Jesse had been burning up the rodeo circuit, determined to take the man's place and gain even more notoriety for the Lost Boys, a local group of cowboy daredevils who were taking the rodeo circuit by storm, winning titles and charming fans all across the country.

Wild. Fearless. Careless.

He was all three and then some.

Her gaze shifted to the face hidden beneath the brim of a worn Stetson. While she couldn't see his eyes thanks to the shadow, she knew they were a deep, mesmerizing violet framed by thick sable lashes. A few days' growth of beard covered his jaw and crept down his neck. Dark brown hair brushed his collar and made her fingers itch to reach out and touch.

"If I were you, I'd stop staring and put my tongue back in my mouth before somebody stomps on it."

The voice startled her, and she turned to see the ancient cowboy who came up beside her.

Eli McGinnis was an old-school wrangler in his late seventies with a head full of snow-white hair that had been slicked back with pomade. His handlebar mustache twitched and she knew he was smiling even though she couldn't actually see the expression beneath the elaborate do on his top lip.

"You'd do well to stop droolin', too," he added. "We got enough mud puddles around here already. A few shit piles, too."

"I wasn't—"

"Drooling?" he cut in. "While I ain't the brightest bulb in the tanning bed, I know drooling when I see it and, lemme tell ya, it ain't attractive on a fine upstanding public servant like yourself. Then again, you ain't actually the mayor yet, so I guess I should be talking to your uncle when it comes to serious public-health issues."

"Uncle E.J. already left for Port Aransas. He and my aunt just bought a house there." Her brow wrinkled as the impact of his words hit. "A public-health issue?" The notion killed the lingering image of Jesse and snagged her complete attention. "What health issue?" A dozen possibilities raced through her mind, from a city-wide epidemic of salmonella to a flesh-eating zombie virus.

Okay, so she spent her evenings watching a little too much cable TV since Charlie had moved into the dorms at the University of Texas last year. A girl had to have *some* fun.

Anxiety raced up her spine. "It's mercury in the water, isn't it?" Fear coiled and tightened in the pit of her stomach. "E. coli in the lettuce crops? Don't tell me Big Earl Jessup is making moonshine in his garage again." At ninety-one, Big Earl was the town's oldest resident, and the most dangerous. He came from a time when the entrepreneurial spirit meant whipping up black diamond whiskey in the backyard and hand-selling it at the annual peach festival. Those days were long gone but that hadn't stopped Big Earl from firing up last year to cook a batch to give away for Christmas. And then again at Easter. And for the Fourth of July.

"You got bigger problems than an old man cooking up moonshine in his deer blind, that's for damn sure."

"Big Earl's cooking in his deer blind?"

Eli frowned. "Stop trying to change the subject. We've got a crisis on our hands."

"Which is?"

"Fake cheese on the nachos. Why, the diner used to put a cup of real whole-milk cheddar on all the nacho platters, but now they're tryin' to cut costs, so they switched to the artificial stuff."

"Fake cheese," she repeated, relief sweeping through her. "That's the major health concern?"

"Damn straight. Why, I was up all night with indigestion. As the leader of this fine community—" he wagged a finger at her "—it's your job to clean it up."

O-kay.

"I'll, um, stop by the diner and see what I can do."

He threw up his hands. "That's all I'm askin', little lady."

Her gaze shifted back to Jesse, who now stood on the other side of the arena talking to two men she didn't recognize. They weren't real working cowboys but rather the slick, wealthy types who flew in every now and then to buy or sell livestock. With their designer boots and high-dollar hats, they probably intimidated most men, but not Jesse. He held his own, a serious look on his face as he motioned to the black bull thrashing around a nearby stall.

"That boy's too damned big for his britches sometimes," Eli muttered.

Her gaze dropped and her breath caught. Actually, he filled out said britches just right.

She watched as he untied his chaps and tossed them over a nearby railing, leaving nothing but a tight pair of faded denims that clung to him like a second skin, outlining his sinewy thighs and trim waist and tight, round butt—

"It's mighty nice of you to come out and warn him." Her gaze snapped up and she glanced at the old man next to her. "Even if he don't realize it."

"It's fine." She shrugged. "It's not like I stop by every day."

Not anymore.

But for those blissful three weeks before they'd graduated, she'd been a permanent fixture on the corral fence, watching him every afternoon after school. Snapping pictures of him. Dreaming of the day when she could leave Lost Gun behind and turn her hobby into a passion.

She'd wanted out of this map dot just as bad as he had. Then.

And now.

She stiffened against the sudden thought. She was happy with her life here. Content.

And even if she wasn't, it didn't matter. She was here. She was staying. End of story.

"Still, you didn't have to go to so much trouble," Eli went on.

"Just looking out for my soon-to-be constituents." No way did Gracie want to admit that she'd come because she still cared about Jesse. Because she still dreamed of him. Because she still *wanted* him.

No, this was about doing the right thing to make up for the wrong she'd done so long ago. She'd had her chance to warn him the first time, and she'd chickened out for fear that seeing him would crumble her resolve and resurrect the wild child she'd been so desperate to bury.

She'd lived with the guilt every day since.

"Tell him to be careful." She took one last look at Jesse, fought against the emotion that churned down deep and walked away.

"THAT MAGAZINE ARTICLE was right about you. You sure put on one helluva show." The words were followed by a steady *clap-clap-clap* as Billy Chisholm, Jesse's youngest brother, walked toward him. Billy was four years younger and eagerly chasing the buckle Jesse had won just last year. "I particularly liked that little twist you did when you flew into the air." He grinned. "Right before you busted your tail."

Jesse glared. "I'm not in the mood."

"I wouldn't be either if I'd just ate it in front of everyone and the horse they rode in on."

But Jesse wasn't concerned about everyone. Just a certain buttoned-up city official with incredible blue eyes.

He barely resisted the urge to steal one last look at her. Not that he hadn't seen her over the years when he'd happened into town—across a crowded main street, through the dingy windows of the local feed store. It was just that those times had been few and far between because Jesse hated Lost Gun as much as the town hated him, and so he'd kept his distance.

But this was different.

She'd been right in front of him. Close enough to touch. To feel. He could still smell her—the warm, luscious scent of vanilla cupcakes topped with a mountain of frosting.

Sweet.

Decadent.

Enough to make him want to cross the dusty arena separating them, pull her into his arms and see if she tasted half as good as he remembered.

Want.

Yep, he still wanted her, all right. The thing was, he didn't *want* to want her, because she sure as hell didn't want him.

He'd thought so at one time. She'd smiled and flirted and rubbed up against him, and he'd foolishly thought she was into him. He'd been a hormone-driven eighteen-year-old back then and he'd fallen hard and fast.

He was a grown-ass man now and a damn sight more experienced. Enough to know that Gracie Stone was nothing special in the big scheme of things. There were dozens of women out there, and Jesse indulged in more than his fair share. And while they all tasted as sweet as could be at first, the sweetness always faded. The sex soon lost its edge. And then Jesse cut ties and moved on to the next.

"…can't remember the last time you bit the bullet

like that," Billy went on. "What the hell happened? Did someone slap you with a ten-pound bag of stupid?"

Okay, maybe Gracie was a little special. She'd been the only woman in his past to break things off with him first, *before* he'd had a chance to lose interest.

He would have, he reminded himself.

Guaran-damn-teed.

From the corner of his eye, he watched her disappear around the holding pens. The air rushed back into his lungs, but his muscles didn't ease.

He was still uptight. Hot. Bothered.

Stupid.

He stiffened and focused on untying the gloves from his hands.

"Alls I can say is thanks, bro," Billy went on. "I bet a wad of cash on your ride just now. My truck payment, as a matter of fact."

Jesse arched an eyebrow. "And you're thanking me for losing your shirt?"

Billy clapped him on the shoulder and sent an ache through his bruised body. "I didn't bet *on* you, bro. I bet *against* you." He winked. "Saw that little gal come round the corner and I knew things were going to get mighty interesting."

Forget stupid. He was pissed.

"She came to warn me," Jesse bit out, his mouth tight. "They're shooting a 'Where Are They Now?' special next week," he told his brother. "A follow-up to *Famous Texas Outlaws.*"

Billy's grin faltered for a split second. "You okay with that?"

Jesse shrugged. "I can handle my fair share of reporters. You know that."

"True enough." Billy nodded before sliding him a sideways glance. "But if you want a little peace and quiet, you can always send them my way." He winked and his grin was back. "I like getting my picture taken."

Billy had been fourteen at the time and excited about being in the limelight. He hadn't been the least bit unnerved by the endless questions about their father's death six years prior, because he'd been too young to really comprehend the gravity of what Silas Chisholm had done. Too young to remember the police and the accusations and the desperate search to recover the money that their father had stolen. Rather, he'd seen the media circus as a welcome distraction from an otherwise shitty life.

"Gracie wants me to lie low," Jesse added. "She thinks it'll help the town."

"And here I thought she came all the way out here because she wanted a piece of PBR's reigning champion."

If only.

Jesse stuffed his gloves into his pocket and fought the longing that coiled inside of him.

Gracie Stone was off-limits.

She'd broken his heart and while it was all water under the bridge now, he had no intention of paddling upstream ever again.

Then again, it wasn't his heart that had stirred the moment he'd come face-to-face with her again. Despite the years that had passed, the chemistry was still as strong as ever.

Stronger, in fact.

And damned if that realization didn't bother him even more than the fact that he'd just landed on his ass in front of an arena full of cowboys. Since Tater Tot had been the ornery bull responsible, he'd just become that much more valuable to the two buyers now waiting inside Jesse's office in a nearby building.

So maybe Gracie's visit wasn't a complete bust after all.

"I've got papers to sign." He motioned to the glass-walled office that overlooked the corral. "Get your gear and get in the chute if you want a turn on Tater Tot before they pack him up and ship him out. And you'd better make it quick because we've got a tuxedo fitting in a half hour and the clock's ticking."

"Sure thing, bro." A grin cut loose from ear to ear. "After that piss-poor display, somebody's gotta show you how it's done."

3

IT TOOK EVERY ounce of willpower Gracie had to bypass the one and only bakery in Lost Gun and head for the town square.

Sure, she eased up on the gas pedal and powered down her window to take in the delicious scent of fresh-baked goodies as she rolled past Sarah's Sweets, but still. She didn't slam on the brakes and make a bee-line for the overflowing counter inside. No red velvet cupcakes or buttercream-frosted sugar cookies for this girl. And no—repeat *no*—Double-Fudge Fantasy Brownies rich in trans fat and high in cholesterol.

Which explained why her hands still trembled and her stomach fluttered when she walked into City Hall.

"How's my favorite mayor-elect?" asked the thirty-something bleached blonde sitting behind the desk in the outer office with a chocolate Danish in front of her.

Longing clawed down deep inside of Gracie, but she tamped it back down. "Fine."

"Methinks you are one terrible liar." Trina Lovett popped a bite of pastry into her mouth and washed it down with a sip of black coffee.

Trina had been working for Gracie's uncle—the current mayor—since she'd graduated high school sixteen years ago—four years before Gracie. Trina had been part of a rise-above-your-environment program that helped young people from impoverished homes—a trailer on the south end of town in Trina's case—find jobs.

He'd hit the jackpot with Trina, who was not only a hard worker but knew everything about everybody. She'd been instrumental in the past few elections— particularly in a too-close-for-comfort runoff with the local sheriff a few years back. E.J. had won, of course, due to his compassionate nature and Trina's connections down at the local honky-tonk. The young woman had bought five rounds of beers the day of the election and earned the forty-two votes needed to win.

Trina had also been instrumental in the most recent campaign, which had seen Gracie take the mayoral race by a landslide.

In exactly two weeks to the day, Gracie Elizabeth Stone would take the sacred oath and step up as the town's first female mayor.

Two weeks, three hours and forty-eight minutes.

Not that she was counting.

"You saw Jesse, didn't you?" When Gracie nodded, Trina's bright red lips parted in a smile. "Tell me *everything.* I caught him on the ESPN channel a few weeks back, but all I could see was a distant view of him straddling a bull for dear life." She wiggled her eyebrows. "What I wouldn't have given to be that bull."

"You work for a public official. You know that, right?"

"Don't get your granny panties in a wad. It's not like

I'm tweeting it or posting to my Facebook status. This is a private conversation." She beamed. "*So?* What's he really like up close? Does he still have those broad shoulders? That great ass?"

Yes and *yes*.

She stiffened and focused on leafing through the stack of mail on Trina's desk. "I'd, um, say he's aged well."

"Seriously? I suppose you look ready to scarf an entire box of cupcakes because of some cowboy who's *aged well?*"

"I suppose he's still hot, if you're into that sort of thing."

"I am." Trina beamed. "I most definitely am."

Gracie frowned. "Not that it makes a difference. I went there strictly in an official capacity. I went. I spoke. He heard. End of story."

Trina regarded her for a long, assessing moment. "He told you to get lost, didn't he?"

"No." The brave face she'd put on faltered. "Yes. I mean, he didn't say it outright—there were no distinct verbs or colorful nouns—but he might as well have."

"Ouch." Her gaze swept Gracie from head to toe and she pursed her bright red lips. "But I can't say as I blame him. You look like you're going to Old Man Winthrow's wake."

"I do black for funerals. This is navy."

"Same thing." She gave Gracie another visual sweep with her assessing blue eyes. "Listen here, girlfriend, men don't take time out of their day to notice navy. It takes a hot color to keep a man from tossing you out on your keister. Red. Neon pink. Even a print—like cheetah or zebra. Something that says you've got a sex drive and you know how to use it. And the skimpier, the better, too. Show a little leg. Some cleavage. Men like cleavage. It gets their full attention every time."

"For the last time—this wasn't a social visit." Gracie eyed Trina's black leather miniskirt. "I'm a public figure. I can't prance around looking like an extra from *Jersey Shore*. Besides, he hates me, and a dress—skimpy or not—isn't going to change that."

"I'm telling you, a good dress is like magic. Slip it on and it'll transform you from a stuffy politician into a major slut. You do remember how much fun being a little slutty can be, don't you?"

As if she could ever forget.

She'd been the baddest girl in high school with the worst reputation, and she'd liked it. She'd liked doing the unexpected and following her gut and having some fun. And she'd *really* liked Jesse James Chisholm.

So much so that she'd been ready to put off attending the University of Texas—her uncle's alma mater—to follow Jesse onto the rodeo circuit. To continue their wild ride together, cheer him on and take enough live-action shots to launch her dream career as a photographer.

But then Jackson had been killed, and Charlie had stopped talking for six months. She'd realized then that she couldn't just turn her back on her little sister and go her own way as her brother had done after their parents had died. Charlie needed her.

And she needed Charlie.

So she'd packed up her camera and her dreams and started playing it safe. She'd followed in her uncle's footsteps, securing a business degree before taking a position as city planner.

Meanwhile, Jesse had ridden every bull from here to Mexico.

They were worlds apart now, and when they did happen to land within a mile radius of each other, the animosity was enough to keep the wall between them thick. Impenetrable.

Animosity because not only had Gracie stood him up on the night they were supposed to leave, but she'd refused to talk to him about it, terrified that if she heard his voice or saw him up close, her determination would crumble. Fearful that the bad girl inside of her would rear her ugly head and lust would get the better of her.

Lust, not love.

She hadn't been able to leave with Jesse, and she'd refused to ask him to give up his life's dream to stay with her in a town that had caused him nothing but pain, and so she'd done the best thing for both of them—she'd broken off all contact.

And her silence had nearly cost him his career.

Not this time.

She'd given him fair warning about the inevitable influx of reporters and now she could get back to work and, more important, forget how good he smelled and how his eyes darkened to a deep, fathomless shade of purple whenever he looked at her.

She fought down the sudden yearning that coiled inside of her. "I don't do slut anymore," she told her assistant.

"Duh." Trina shrugged. "You've been wearing those Spanx so long, you've forgotten how to peel them off and cut loose."

If only.

But that was the trouble in a nutshell. She'd never

really forgotten. Deep in her heart, in the dead of night, she remembered what it felt like to live for the moment, to feel the rush of excitement, to walk on the wild side. It felt good—so freakin' *good*—and she couldn't help but want to feel that way again.

Just once.

Not that she was acting on that want. No way. No how. No sirree. Charlie needed a home and the people of Lost Gun needed a mayor, and Gracie needed to keep her head on straight and her thoughts out of the gutter.

"So what's on the agenda today?" she blurted, eager to get them back onto a safer subject. "City council meeting? Urgent political strategy session? Constituent meet and greet?" She needed something—anything—to get her mind off Jesse James Chisholm and the fact that he'd looked every bit as good as she remembered. And then some. "Surely Uncle E.J. left a big pile of work before he headed for Port Aransas to close on the new house?"

"Let's see." Trina punched a few buttons on her computer. "You're in luck. You've got a meeting with Mildred Jackson from the women's sewing circle— she wants the city to commission a quilt for your new office."

"That's it?"

"That and a trip to the animal shelter." When Gracie arched an eyebrow, Trina added, "I've been reading this article online about politicians and their canine friends. Do you know that a dog ups your favorability rating by five percent?"

"I already have a dog."

"A ball of fluff who humps everything in sight

doesn't count." When Gracie gave her a sharp look, she shrugged. "Not that I have anything against humping, but you've got a reputation to think of. A horny mutt actually takes away poll points."

"Sugar Lips isn't a mutt. She's a maltipom. Half Maltese. Half Pomeranian." Trina gave her a *girlfriend, pu-leeze* look and she added, "I've got papers to prove it."

"Labs and collies polled at the top with voters, and the local shelter just happens to have one of each," Trina pressed. "Just think how awesome it will look when the new mayor-elect waltzes in on Adopt-a-Pet Day and picks out her new Champ or Spot."

"Don't tell me—Champ and Spot were top-polling animal names?"

"Now you're catching on."

Gracie shook her head. "I can't just bring home another dog. Sugar will freak. She has control issues."

"Think of the message it will send to voters. Image is everything."

As if she didn't know that. She'd spent years trying to shake her own bad image, to bury it down deep, to make people forget, and she'd finally succeeded. Twelve long years later, she'd managed to earn the town's loyalty. Their trust.

Now it was just a matter of keeping it.

She shrugged. "Okay, I'll get another dog."

"And a date," Trina added. "That way people can also envision you as the better half of a couple, i.e., family oriented."

"Where do you get this stuff?"

"PerfectPolitician.com. They say if you want to project a stable, reliable image, you need to be in a stable, reliable relationship. I was thinking we should call Chase Carter. He's president of the bank, not to mention a huge campaign contributor. He's also president of the chamber of commerce and vice president of the zoning commission."

And about as exciting as the 215-page car-wash proposition just submitted by the president of the Ladies' Auxiliary for next year's fundraiser.

Gracie eyed her assistant. "Isn't Chase gay?"

"A small technicality." Trina waved a hand. "This is about image, not getting naked on the kitchen table. I know he isn't exactly a panty dropper like Jesse James Chisholm, but—"

"Call him." Chase *wasn't* Jesse, which made him perfect dating material. He wouldn't be interested in getting her naked and she wouldn't be interested in getting him naked. And she certainly wouldn't sit around fantasizing about the way his thigh muscles bunched when he crossed a rodeo arena.

She ignored the faint scent of dust and leather that still lingered on her clothes and shifted her attention to something safe. "Do you know anything about Big Earl Jessup?" She voiced the one thing besides Jesse Chisholm and his scent that had been bothering her since she'd left the training arena.

"I know he's too old to be your date. That and he's got hemorrhoids the size of boulders." Gracie's eyes widened and Trina shrugged. "News travels fast in a small town. Bad news travels even faster."

"I don't want to go out with him. I heard through the grapevine that he might be cooking moonshine in his deer blind."

Trina's eyebrow shot up. "The really good kind he used to make for the annual peach festival?"

"Maybe."

"Hot damn." When Gracie cut her a stare, she added, "I mean, *damn.* What a shame."

"Exactly. He barely got off by the skin of his teeth the last time he was brought up on charges. Judge Ellis is going to throw the book at him if he even thinks that Big Earl is violating his parole."

"Isn't Big Earl like a hundred?"

"He's in his nineties."

"What kind of dipshit would throw a ninetysomething in prison?"

"The dipshit whose car got blown up the last time Big Earl was cooking. Judge Ellis had a case of the stuff in his trunk at the annual Fourth of July picnic. A Roman candle got too close and bam, his Cadillac went up in flames."

"Isn't that his own fault for buying the stuff?"

"That's what Uncle E.J. said, which was why Big Earl got off on probation. But Judge Ellis isn't going to be swayed again. He'll nail him to the wall." And stir another whirlwind of publicity when Lost Gun became home to the oldest prison inmate. At least that was what Uncle E.J. had said when he'd done his best to keep the uproar to a minimum.

"I need to find out for sure," Gracie told Trina.

"If you go nosying around Big Earl's place, you're liable to get shot. Tell you what—I'll drop by his place after I get my nails done. My daddy used to buy from him all the time when I was a little girl. I'll tell him I just stopped by for old times' sake. So what do you think?" She held up two-inch talons. "Should I go with wicked red or passionate pink this time?"

"Don't you usually get your nails done on Friday?"

"Hazel over at the motel called and said two reporters from Houston are checking in this afternoon and I want to look my best before the feeding frenzy starts."

"Reporters?" Alarm bells sounded in Gracie's head and a rush of adrenaline shot through her. "Already?"

Trina nodded. "She's got three more checking in tomorrow. And twenty-two members of the Southwest chapter of the Treasure Hunters Alliance. Not to mention, Lyle over at the diner called and said the folks from the Whispering Winds Senior Home stopped by for lunch today. They usually go straight through to Austin for their weekly shopping trip, but one of them read a preview about the documentary in the TV listings and now everybody wants to check out Silas Chisholm's old stomping grounds. A few of them even brought their gardening trowels for a little digging after lunch."

"But there's nothing to find." According to police reports, the wad of cash from Silas Chisholm's bank heist had gone up in flames with the man himself.

"That's what Lyle told them, but you know folks don't listen. They'd rather think there's some big windfall just waiting to be discovered." Which was exactly what the documentary's host had been banking on when he'd brought up the missing money and stirred a whirlwind of doubt all those years ago.

Maybe the money hadn't gone up in flames.

Maybe, just maybe, it was still out there waiting to be discovered. To make someone rich.

"I should head over to the diner and set them all straight."

"Forget it. I saved you a trip and stopped by myself on my way in." Trina waved a hand. "Bought them all a complimentary round of tapioca, and just like that, they forgot all about treasure hunting. Say, why don't you come with me to the salon?"

"I can't. The remodeling crew will be here first thing tomorrow and I promised I'd have everything picked out by then."

It was a lame excuse, but the last thing she needed was to sit in the middle of a nail salon and endure twenty questions about her impromptu visit with Jesse Chisholm and the impending media circus.

"That and I still need to unpack all the boxes from my old office."

"Suit yourself, but I'd take advantage of the light schedule between now and inauguration time. You'll be up to your neck in city business soon enough once you take your oath."

A girl could only hope.

Trina glanced at her watch and pushed up from her desk. "I'm outta here." Her gaze snagged on the phone and she smiled. "Right after I hook you up with Mr. Wrong, that is."

She punched in a number on the phone. "Hey, Sally. It's Trina over at the mayor's office. Is Chase in?…The mayor-elect would like to invite him to be her escort for the inauguration ceremony.…What? He's hosting a pottery class right now?…No, no, don't interrupt him. Just tell him the mayor-elect called and wants to sweep him off his feet.…Yeah, yeah, she loves pottery, too.…"

Gracie balled her fingers to keep from pressing the

disconnect button, turned and headed for the closed door. A date with Chase was just what she needed. He was perfect. Upstanding. Respectable. Boring.

She ignored the last thought and picked up her steps. Hinges creaked and she found herself in the massive office space that would soon be the headquarters of Lost Gun's new mayor.

Under normal circumstances, the new mayor moved into the old mayor's office, but just last week the city had approved budget changes allocating a huge amount to renovate the east wing of City Hall, including the massive space that had once served as a courtroom. Gracie was the first new face they'd elected in years and change was long overdue. She was getting a brand-new office and reception area, as well as her own private bathroom.

Everything had been cleared out and the floors stripped down to the concrete slab. A card table sat off to one side. Her laptop and a spare phone sat on top, along with a stack of paint colors and flooring samples and furniture selections all awaiting her approval. A stack of boxes from her old office filled a nearby corner.

She drew a deep steadying breath and headed for the boxes to decide what to keep and what to toss.

A half hour later she was halfway through the third box when she unearthed a stack of framed pictures. She stared at the first. The last rays of a hot summer's day reflected on the calm water of Lost Gun Lake and a smile tugged at her lips. She could still remember sitting on the riverbank, the grass tickling her toes as she waited for the perfect moment when the lighting would be just right. She'd taken the photograph her freshman year in high school for a local competition. She hadn't won. The prize—a new Minolta camera—had gone to the nephew of one of the judges, who'd done an artsy shot of a rainy day in black-and-white film.

A lesson, she reminded herself. Photography was a crapshoot. Some people made it. Some didn't. And so she'd given it up for something steady. Reliable.

If only her brother had done the same.

But instead, he'd enlisted in the army on his eighteenth birthday, just weeks after their parents had died. He'd gone on to spend four years on the front lines in Iraq while she and Charlie had tried to make a new life in Lost Gun with Uncle E.J. and Aunt Cheryl. But it had never felt quite right.

It had never felt like home.

Her aunt and uncle had been older and set in their ways—acting out of duty rather than love—and so living with them had felt like living in a hotel.

Cold.

Impersonal.

And so Gracie had made up her mind to leave right after graduation, to make her own way and forget the tragedy that had destroyed her family. She'd snapped picture after picture and dreamed of bigger and better things far away from Lost Gun. But then Jackson had died and Charlie had become clingy and fearful. She'd followed Gracie everywhere, even into bed at night, terrified that fate would take her older sister the way it had snatched up their brother.

Gracie couldn't blame her. She'd felt the same crippling fear when their parents had died. She'd reached out for Jackson, but he'd left and so she'd had no one to soothe the uncertainty, to give her hope.

She stuffed the framed picture back inside the box, along with a dozen others that had lined the walls of her city planner's office, and reached for a Sharpie. Once upon a time, she'd hated the idea of tossing them when they could easily serve as cheap decoration, and so she'd kept them.

No more.

With trembling fingers, she scribbled Storage on the outside and moved on to the next box loaded with old files.

She rifled through manila folders for a full thirty minutes before she found herself thinking about Jesse and how good he'd looked and the way he'd smelled and—

Ugh. She needed something to get her mind back on track.

Maybe a brownie or a cupcake or a frosted cookie—

She killed the dangerous thought, grabbed her purse and headed out the door. Forget waiting on Trina. She would head out and check on Big Earl herself, and she wouldn't—repeat, *would not*—stop at the bakery on the way. She'd cleaned up her eating habits right along with everything else when she'd decided to play it safe and stop being so wild and reckless.

And *safe* meant looking both ways when she crossed the street and wearing her seat belt when she climbed behind the wheel and eating right. She had her health to think of and so she followed a strict low-carb, low-sugar, low-fat diet high in protein and fiber. That meant no brownies, no matter how desperate the craving.

No sirree, she wasn't falling off the wagon.

Not even if Jesse himself stripped naked right in front of her and she desperately needed something—

anything—to sate her hunger and keep her hands off of him.

Okay, so maybe if he stripped *naked*.

A very vivid image of Jesse pushed into her thoughts and she saw him standing on the creek bed, the moonlight playing off his naked body. Her lips tingled and her nipples tightened and she picked up her steps.

No *naked* and no brownies.

4

GRACIE PULLED TO a stop in front of the bakery over an hour later and killed the engine.

She wasn't going to blow her diet with a brownie. She was headed straight for the health food store next door and a carob cookie with tofu frosting or a bran muffin with yogurt filling or *something*. A healthy alternative with just a teeny tiny ounce of sweetness to help steady her frantic heartbeat after the visit to Big Earl's place.

She hadn't actually had a face-to-face with the man himself, but she had come this close to being ripped to shreds by his dogs.

Charlie would freak fifty ways till Sunday if she found out. Luckily, she'd moved into the dorms at the University of Texas last year and so Gracie didn't have to worry about explaining the ripped hem of her skirt or the dirt smears on her blouse. At least not until this weekend when her little sis came home for her weekly visit and caught wind of the gossip.

If she came home.

She'd canceled the past three weeks in a row with

one excuse after the other—she was studying; she had a date; she wanted to hit the latest party.

Not that Gracie was counting. She knew Charlie would much rather go out with friends than make homemade pizza with her older sister. Charlie was growing up, pulling away, and that was good. Still, when her little sister finally did make it home, Gracie would be here.

She would always be here.

Because that's what home meant. It was permanent. Steady. Reliable.

Her gaze swiveled to the two old men nursing a game of dominoes in front of the hardware store directly across the street.

At ninety-three, Willard and Jacob Amberjack were the oldest living twins in the county. And the nosiest.

She debated making a quick trip home to change, but that would put her back at the health food store after hours and she needed something now—even something disgustingly healthy.

She drew a deep breath, braced herself for the impending encounter and climbed out of her car.

"Don't you look like something the dog just dragged in," Jacob called out the moment her feet touched pavement. "What in tarnation happened to you?"

"Was it a hit-and-run?" Willard leaned forward in his rocking chair. "Was it a car? A truck? Or maybe you got molested." He pointed a bony finger at his brother. "I been tellin' Jacob here that the world's goin' to hell in a handbasket."

"It wasn't a hit-and-run. And I wasn't molested," she rushed on, eager to set the record straight before their tongues started wagging. "I was just cleaning out my office and I snagged my skirt on a loose nail."

"You sure? 'Cause there's no shame if'n' you was molested. Things happen. Why, old Myrtle Nell over at the VFW hall accosted me just last night on account of I'm the best dancer in the place and she really wanted to waltz. Had to let her down easy and I can tell you, she was none too happy about it. Poor thing headed straight home, into a bottle of Metamucil. Ain't heard from her since."

"That's terrible."

"Damn straight. Everybody knows there ain't no substitute for good ole-fashioned prune juice."

O-kay. "Enjoy your game, fellas." Before they could launch into any more speculation, Gracie put her back to the curious old men and stepped up onto the curb.

"Afternoon, Miss Gracie."

"Hey there, Miss Gracie."

"See you at the church bake sale tomorrow, Miss Gracie."

"I wouldn't miss it for the world," she told the trio of women who exited the bake shop, glossy pink boxes clutched in their manicured hands.

The youngest one, a thirtyish soccer mom by the name of Carleen Harwell, held up two of the boxes that emanated a yummy smell. "Sarah donated ten dozen Rice Krispies Treats."

"Excellent." She waved as the women headed down the street and said hello to a few more people passing by before turning her attention to the display case that filled the massive storefront window. Dozens of pies lined the space, along with a sign that read It's Pick Your Pie Tuesday!

Not that she was going to pick a pie. Or a cake. Or anything else tempting her from the other side of the glass. But looking… There suddenly seemed nothing wrong with that.

"Go for the chocolate meringue."

The deep, familiar voice vibrated along her nerve endings. Heat whispered along her senses. Her stomach hollowed out.

"Or the Fudge Ecstasy. That's one of my personal favorites."

Excitement rippled up her spine, followed by a wave of *oh, no* because Jesse James Chisholm was the last person she needed to see right now.

He was the reason she was so worked up in the first place. So anxious. And desperate. And hungry.

Really, really hungry.

Run! her gut screamed. *Before you do something stupid like turn around and talk to him.*

"If memory serves—" the words slid past her lips as she turned "—you were always partial to cherry." So much for listening to her instincts. "In fact, I seem to recall you wolfing down an entire cherry cobbler at the Travis County Fair and Rodeo." She didn't mean to bring up their first date, but her mouth seemed to have a mind all its own. "With two scoops of ice cream on the side."

"Miss Hazel's prizewinning cobbler," he said, a grin tugging at his lips as the memory surfaced. "That woman sure can bake."

"So can Sarah." Gracie motioned to the display case and the golden lattice-topped cherry pie sitting center stage. Inside gold certificates and blue ribbons lined a nearby wall, along with an autographed picture of

Tom Cruise in his *Risky Business* heyday. "So why the switch to chocolate?"

"When I was laid up after Diamond Dust, Billy thought he'd cheer me up with some fresh-picked cherries from Old Man Winthrow's tree. I ate the entire basket in one sitting and made myself sick. I've been boycotting ever since."

"I don't do chocolate," she announced. She didn't mean to keep the conversation going. She had a strict no-talk policy where Jesse was concerned. And a no-closeness policy, too. Because when she got too close, she couldn't help but talk.

Which explained why she'd avoided him altogether for the past twelve years.

No talking. No touching. No kissing. No—

"I mean, I like chocolate—brownies, in particular," she blurted, eager to do something with her mouth that didn't involve planting a great big one smack-dab on his lips, "but I don't actually eat any."

"What happened to the Hershey's-bar-a-day habit?"

"I kicked it. I'm into healthy eating now. No Hershey's bars or brownies or anything else with processed sugar. I'm headed to the health food store." She motioned to the sign shaped like a giant celery stalk just to her left. "They make an all-natural apple tart. It has a cornflake crust. It's really delicious."

"Cornflakes, huh?" He didn't look convinced.

She couldn't blame him. She remembered the small sample she'd tasted the last time she'd been inside the Green Machine and her throat tightened. "Delicious might be pushing it. But it's decent." She shrugged. "Besides, deprivation is good for the soul. It builds character."

"It also makes you more likely to blow at the first sign of temptation."

And how.

Twelve years and counting.

"Everything all right, Miss Gracie?" Jacob Amberjack's voice carried across the street and drew her attention.

"It's fine." She waved at the old man and his brother.

"'Cause if that there feller's the one what assaulted you, Willard here would be happy to come over there and defend your honor."

"I didn't assault her," Jesse told the two men.

The old man glared. "Tell it to the judge, Chisholm."

"No one's telling anything to anyone, because nothing happened," Gracie said.

"That ain't the way we see it," the two men said in unison.

"I'd give it a rest if I were you," Jesse advised.

"We ain't afraid of you, Chisholm. There might be snow on the roof, but there's plenty of fire in the cookstove. Willard here—" Jacob motioned next to him "—will rip you a new one—"

"How come I'm the one who always has to do the rippin'?" Willard cut in. "Hell's bells, I can barely move as it is. You know I got a bad back."

"Well, I got bunions."

"So? You ain't fightin' with your feet...."

The two men turned their focus to each other and Gracie's gaze shifted back to Jesse. She expected the anger. The hatred. He'd been big on both way back when, particularly when it came to the citizens of Lost Gun. He'd hated them as much as they'd hated him, and he'd never been shy about showing it.

Instead of hard, glittering anger, she saw a flash of pain, a glimmer of regret, and she had the startling thought that while he looked every bit the hard, bulletproof cowboy she remembered so well, there was a softening in his gaze. His heart.

As if Jesse actually cared what the two old men had said to him.

As if.

No, Jesse James Chisholm didn't give two shakes what the fine people of Lost Gun thought about him. He hated the town and he always would.

Meanwhile, she was stuck smack-dab in the middle of it.

She ignored the depressing thought and searched for her voice. "So, um, what are you doing here?"

He motioned to the bridal salon just two doors down. "I have to see a man about a tux. I'm Pete's right hand."

"I didn't mean here as in this location. I meant—" she motioned between them "—*here.* You couldn't wait to get away from me earlier. Now you're standing here having a conversation. Because?"

He frowned, as if he didn't quite understand it any more than she did. "You caught me at a bad time, I suppose."

"I didn't mean to. I just wanted to warn you before the reporters beat me to it."

"You did the right thing."

"I just thought you should know…" Her gaze snapped up. "What did you just say?"

"It's not about what I just said. It's about what I *should* have said earlier." His gaze caught and held hers. "Thanks for giving me the heads-up." Where she'd missed the gratitude that morning, there was no mistaking the sentiment now. "Motives aside, you warned me and I am grateful."

"Me, too." When he gave her a questioning look, she added, "For the flowers that you sent when my brother died. I should have said thank you back then. I didn't."

"I'm really sorry about what happened to him."

"It was his choice." She shrugged. "He enlisted. He knew the risks, but he took them anyway."

"Seems to me," he said after a long moment, "he died doing something he believed in. I can't think of a better way to go myself."

Neither could she at that moment and oddly enough, the tightness in her chest eased just a fraction. "If you're not careful, you'll be following in his footsteps. That was a hard fall you took back at the arena."

A wicked grin tugged at the corner of his lips. "The harder, the better."

"I'm talking about riding."

"So am I, sugar." The grin turned into a full-blown smile. "So am I." The words were like a chisel chipping away at the wall she'd erected between them. Even more, he stared deep into her eyes and for a long moment, she forgot everything.

The nosy men sitting across the street. The endless stream of people walking past. The all-important fact that she needed to get a move on if she meant to get inside the health food store before they closed.

He made her feel like the only woman in the world.

Which was crazy with a big fat *C*.

He was flirting, for heaven's sake. Just the kind of sexy, seductive innuendo she would expect from one of the hottest bachelors on the PBR circuit.

It wasn't as if he wanted to sweep her up and ride off

into the sunset. This wasn't about her personally. She was simply one of many in a long, long line of women who lusted after him, and he was simply living up to his reputation.

Just as she should be living up to hers.

She stiffened. "It was nice to see you, but I really should get going. I've got a ton of work back at City Hall."

"Duty calls, right?"

Her gaze collided with his and she could have sworn she saw a glimmer of disappointment before it disappeared into the vivid violet depths. "Always."

And then she turned and hurried toward the Green Machine before she did the unthinkable—like wrap her arms around him, hop on and ride him for a scorching eight seconds in front of God and the Amberjack twins.

She would have done just that prior to her brother's death, but she was no longer the rebellious teenager desperate to flee the confines of her small town.

She was mature.

Responsible.

Safe.

If only that thought didn't depress her almost as much as the skinny treats that waited for her inside the health food store.

5

"THIS IS JUST plain wrong." Cole Unger Chisholm frowned as he stood on the raised dais in the middle of the mirrored dressing room of Lost Gun's one and only bridal salon. "Tell me again why I have to wear this."

"For Pete." Jesse ignored the prickly fabric of his own tuxedo and tried to forget the sugary scent of vanilla cupcakes that still teased his nostrils. Of all the people he could possibly run into—the local police chief, the busybodies from the Ladies' Auxiliary, the gossipy Amberjack brothers—it had to be Gracie. Talk about rotten luck.

"Stop your bellyaching," he told Cole. "You're wearing it and that's that."

"Pete don't give two licks about a freakin' tuxedo with a girly purple cummerbund and matching tie, so why should I?"

"Because he's marrying Wendy and she does give two licks." Jesse lifted one arm so Mr. McGinnis, the shop's owner and tailor, could adjust the hem on his sleeve.

Cole eyed his reflection. "But the cummerbund looks almost pink."

"It's actually lavender." The comment came from the petite blonde who appeared in the curtained doorway. Her blue eyes narrowed as she eyed Cole. "And you're right. It's all wrong."

"See?" Cole pushed back a strand of unruly brown hair and stared defiantly at Jesse. "That's what I've been saying all along."

"You've got it hooked in the front," Wendy announced. "It's supposed to hook in the back. Isn't that right, Mr. McGinnis?"

"Sure enough, Miss Wendy." The older man slipped the last pin into Jesse's hem and turned to work on Cole's tux. In a matter of seconds, he readjusted the shiny taffeta material and stepped back. "There. Now it's perfect."

"Perfect?" Cole frowned. "But I look like a—"

"Where's Pete?" Jesse cut in, drawing Wendy's attention before Cole could say something he would later regret.

And Jesse had no doubt his middle brother would do just that. Cole had zero filters when it came to running his mouth, which explained why he ended up in more than his fair share of bar fights.

"He's trying on his tuxedo in the next room," Wendy replied. "He'll be out in a second." She turned a grateful smile on Cole. "Listen, I know you don't feel comfortable all dressed up like this, but I really appreciate it."

"It's our pleasure," Jesse cut in before Cole could open his mouth again.

"Damn straight it is." The comment came from Billy, who waltzed in wearing the same tuxedo.

Wendy turned on the youngest Chisholm and her eyes went misty. "You look wonderful!"

Billy winked. "Anything for you and Pete." He stepped up on the dais next to Cole so that Mr. Mc-Ginnis could work on the hem of his pants. "Ain't that right, bro?" He clapped Cole on the shoulder.

The middle Chisholm shrugged free. "I guess so."

"I was hoping you'd feel that way." Another smile touched Wendy's pink lips and Jesse knew she had something up her sleeve even before she added, "I've been meaning to talk to you, Cole. See, one of my friends is flying in from Houston and I need someone to pick her up at the airport. I would get Red to do it, but Hannah—that's her name—comes in smack-dab during his soap opera time, and you know how that goes."

Red owned the only cab in Lost Gun. He was also a die-hard soap opera fan. Since he was as old as dirt, he hadn't yet discovered TiVo or a DVR, which meant he was completely out of commission between the hours of 11:00 a.m. and 2:00 p.m. on any given weekday.

"She tried to get a different flight," Wendy went on, "but it's the only one that will put her here in time for the rehearsal dinner."

"No problem," Jesse said. "Cole here would be happy to pick her up for you." He clapped his brother on the shoulder, his hand lingering. "Isn't that right?"

"But I've got a training session—" the younger Chisholm started. Jesse dug his fingers into muscle and Cole bit out, "All right, already. I'll do it."

"You will?" Excitement lit Wendy's eyes.

Jesse dug his fingers even deeper and the younger

man blurted, "Sure thing. Family's family," he muttered. "We stick together."

"Great, because I told her all about you and she's dying to meet you."

"Who's dying to meet who?" Pete Gunner walked into the fitting area and slid an arm around his wife-to-be.

"Hannah," Wendy told him. "Ever since she moved to Houston from New York, she's been dying to meet a real cowboy. I told her all about Cole and she's super hyped."

"Wait a second." Cole shrugged loose from Jesse's warning grasp. "Picking her up is one thing, but this sounds like a setup."

"Don't be silly. You don't have to be her date for the wedding."

"That's a relief." Cole tugged at the tie around his neck as if he couldn't quite breathe. "For a second there, I thought you wanted me to babysit her the entire night."

"Of course not." Wendy smiled. "Just sit with her during the reception. And maybe ask her to dance once or twice. Oh, and make sure she gets back to the motel that night and—"

"Pretty much babysit her the whole danged night," Cole cut in. His mouth pulled into a tight line. "Hell's bells. I knew it. It *is* a setup."

"Okay, maybe it is." Wendy shrugged. "But it'll be fun. And speaking of fun, I've got to decide on the actual centerpiece so the florist can finalize the order." She planted a kiss on her groom's lips and headed for a nearby doorway and the endless array of floral arrangements spread out on a table in the next room.

Cole opened his mouth, but Pete held up a hand. "Don't fight it, bro. It'll only make things worse."

"But I can get my own date."

"True, but Wendy doesn't want you bringing one of your usual buckle bunnies to the wedding."

"He's talking about the Barbie triplets," Billy chimed in.

"They're not triplets," Cole said. "They're just sisters who are close in age. And I wasn't going to bring all three. Just Crystal. She's the oldest and the prettiest."

"And the wildest," Pete added, "which is why she's off-limits for the wedding. Wendy thinks you need to meet a nice girl."

"I meet plenty of nice girls." Cole unhooked the cummerbund and handed it to Mr. McGinnis.

"Nice and easy," Billy added.

"What's wrong with easy?"

"Nothing if you're sixteen and horny as hell," the youngest Chisholm pointed out. "You're twenty-nine. You should be thinking about your future."

"Like you?"

"Damn straight." Billy nodded. "As a matter of fact, I've got my own date already lined up for the wedding and I can guarantee her last name isn't Barbie."

"Big Earl Jessup's great-granddaughter is not a date," Cole pointed out. "She's a death wish. She's liable to challenge you to an arm-wrestling match."

"So she's a little rough around the edges," Billy admitted. "She's a tomboy, and that just means we've got a shitload in common. She's interesting."

"And safe," Jesse offered.

"Exactly." Billy unhooked his own tie and handed

it to the tailor. "I'm not looking to settle down, which makes Casey Jessup the perfect date for this wedding. I don't have to worry about her sitting around getting bright ideas from all this hoopla. She's as far from wife material as a woman can get."

"Casey's got a cousin." Cole's gaze shifted to Pete. "I could ask her to the wedding."

"Too late. Wendy got the draw on you and now you've got to man up."

"But I hate fix-ups." He shrugged off his jacket.

"Look on the bright side," Billy added, "Wendy's friend *could* turn out to have a smoking-hot body and zero morals."

Cole shook his head. "You know the odds of that are slim to none."

"True, but it can't hurt to fantasize." Jesse motioned to Billy. "Just like this one outriding me in Vegas in a few weeks."

"That buckle is mine," Billy vowed, trying to wrestle free when Jesse grabbed him in a headlock.

"Keep thinking that and maybe one day you'll knock me out of the running." But not this time. Jesse had been working too long and too hard to go down with just one buckle to his credit. He wanted a second. And a third. Hell, maybe even a fourth.

And then?

He let go of his brother and shifted his attention to the next room and a dreamy-eyed Wendy, who moved from arrangement to arrangement eyeing the various flowers.

For a split second, he saw Gracie leaning over a bouquet of lilies, her eyes sparkling, her full, luscious lips curved into a smile. Fast-forward to another vision of the two of them standing at the altar saying "I do," living happily ever after.

Crazy.

Not the "I do" part, mind you. Jesse wasn't opposed to settling down and having a family. It was the notion of living happily ever after with Gracie Stone that was just plumb loco.

She represented everything he wanted desperately to forget—his past, this town.

He wanted to escape them both. That was why he'd kept his distance all these years.

Why he needed to keep his distance now.

Jesse stiffened and peeled off the tuxedo jacket. "I need to head out." The back way this time. No way was he going to risk another run-in with her out front. She'd smelled so good and looked even more luscious than anything in the front window of the bakery.

And damned if he'd been able to think straight with her right in front of him.

That was why he'd talked to her. Flirted with her. *Crazy.*

"Why don't you come back to the house with me and Wendy?" Pete's voice drew his attention. "Eli's got the cook working on a big spread for supper. The twins are visiting from El Paso. We could make it a family dinner."

The twins were Jimmy and Jake Barber, fast-rising stars on the team-roping circuit and the last two members of the notorious Lost Boys. They'd lived out at Pete's ranch with Jesse and his brothers up until Pete had proposed to Wendy last year. Jesse and the others had gotten together then and decided with Pete settling down and retiring, it was time for the rest of them to spread their wings. The twins had moved up to El Paso. Cole was in Houston. Billy had just bought a few hundred acres outside of Lost Gun and was making plans to build a house of his own. And Jesse had finally bought a spread in Austin.

Now it was just a matter of tying up all the loose ends here—namely selling his stock at the training facility—and moving on.

"Come on," Pete prompted. "It's been forever since we've all sat down together. Maybe Eli will pull out his guitar."

"Sounds tempting, but the drive out will put me back at the motel close to midnight and I need to be up early."

"So stay over at the ranch house. Hell, I don't know why you're cooped up at that motel in the first place."

"Because you're this close to tying the knot, bro. You and Wendy deserve a little privacy." Pete arched an eyebrow and Jesse added, "That way if you guys want to get naked in the dining room or the front parlor, there's nobody stopping you."

Pete looked ready to protest, but then he shrugged. "I suppose a man can't argue with getting naked. So what about you?" He eyed Jesse. "You got a date for the wedding? If not, I'm sure Wendy could rustle up a friend."

"I've got a few possibilities."

"Just make sure none of them work down at Luscious Longhorns—otherwise she'll blow a gasket." Pete grinned for a long moment before his look faded into one of serious intent. "Eli mentioned that Gracie came to see you today."

Jesse nodded. "They're going to re-air the television show."

"When?"

"Tuesday a week."

"Maybe you ought to leave early, then. Head up to Austin and get some extra practice time in before your next rodeo."

"I can practice here just fine. Besides, I've got another buyer coming in to look at a few more bulls in the morning. I want to get them all sold off before I leave. That and there's a little something called a wedding I need to be here for."

"You could always miss it."

Jesse shook his head. "Like hell. I'm your best man."

"And I'm the guy who watched you nurse a few dozen broken bones thanks to a she-devil named Diamond Dust. I have no desire to do it again."

"I was eighteen and gun-shy when it came to the press. I can handle it now. You just worry about getting your sorry hide to the church on Saturday." Jesse grinned. "Because I plan to keep you out plenty late the night before for the bachelor party."

"Thanks, man." Pete clapped him on the back. "I owe you one."

But it was Jesse who owed Pete. The man had saved him and his brothers all those years ago, and no way was Jesse jumping ship on the most important day of Pete's life. He was here and he was staying until the festivities were over.

Even more, he wasn't the same kid who'd been blindsided all those years ago. He dealt with reporters all the time now, not to mention overzealous fans and even the occasional critic. It was just a matter of staying one step ahead.

And he was, thanks to Gracie.

Because she wanted to keep the peace in her small town.

That was the only reason she'd gone to the trouble of warning him. He *knew* that. At the same time, he couldn't shake the crazy hope that maybe, just maybe, she'd wanted to see him.

As much as he'd wanted to see her.

There was no denying the chemistry that still sizzled between them. He'd felt the charge in the air, and so had she. There'd been no mistaking the tremble of her full bottom lip or the glimmer in her eyes. He knew the look even after all these years.

Yep, the chemistry was still there.

Not that it meant anything.

She was still determined to keep her distance—her quick retreat into the health food store proved that— and so was he.

He tamped down a sudden rush of disappointment. "I'd better get going. I want to get in another ride or two before I call it a night." He shed the tie and cummerbund and headed back to the dressing room to retrieve his clothes.

And then Jesse snuck out the back way and turned his attention to the one thing that wasn't beyond his reach—another PBR championship.

6

THIS WAS THE last place he needed to be.

The thought struck later that evening as Jesse pulled into the dirt driveway of the three-acre lot that sat just a few blocks over from City Hall.

He was supposed to be back at the motel, eating takeout and icing his shoulder after a hellacious training session. Or nursing a few beers at the local honky-tonk with his brothers. Or playing a few rounds of pool at one of the beer joints out on the interstate.

Anywhere but here, smack-dab in the middle of the town he so desperately hated.

His gaze pushed through the settling darkness and scanned the area. Once upon a time, reporters had walked every inch of this sad, miserable stretch, picking through the burned ruins that had once been the two-room shack that Jesse and his brothers had shared with their dad. The small single-car garage still sat in the far back corner, the paint peeling, the roof rusted out. His dad's broken-down 1970 Buick sat next to the shell of a building, the doors missing, the frame rusted and rotting.

The shame of Lost Gun.

That was how the newspapers had referred to the Chisholm place when *Famous Texas Outlaws* had aired for the first time on the Discovery Channel.

Not that his dad had been a famous Texas outlaw. Far from it. Silas Chisholm had been a wannabe with a lust for easy money and an aversion to hard work, which was why he'd moved his three young boys to Lost Gun in the first place.

The town had originated as a haven to criminals and gamblers back in the early 1800s. Lost Gun, so named because it was rumored to be home to a pearl-handled Colt once belonging to one of Texas's most notorious outlaws—John Wesley Hardin. The man had supposedly hidden the gun while on the run from Texas Rangers, but other than a colorful legend, there'd never been any actual proof of its existence.

Word of mouth had been enough for a recently widowed Silas to uproot his three sons from Beaumont, Texas, and travel across the state in search of the valuable Colt. When the gun hadn't panned out, Silas had started looking for another big-money opportunity.

Now, remember, son, when things look bad and it looks like you're not gonna make it, then you gotta get mean. I mean plumb mad-dog mean. 'Cause if you lose your head and you give up, then you neither live nor win.

His dad's words echoed in his head. As worthless as the man had been, he'd been just as determined when it came to finding an easy payday. After an endless string of dead-end schemes, he'd turned to the Lost Gun Savings & Loan.

Jesse still wasn't sure how he'd pulled it off, but he'd

actually made off with a quarter of a million dollars. All pissed away when he'd drunk himself into a stupor later that same night. He'd passed out with a cigarette in his mouth that had resulted in a deadly blaze.

He'd died in that fire because Jesse, only thirteen at the time, hadn't been strong enough to drag him off the couch. Even more, the fortune Silas had been so anxious to get his hands on had gone up in flames.

Not that everybody believed the money had perished. Curt Calhoun, the reporter who'd aired the story five years later, had posed so many questions that folks had started to wonder if maybe, just maybe, the money might still be out there. Calhoun's speculation had pulled in every two-bit criminal this side of the Rio Grande, not to mention a shitload of fortune hunters. They'd descended on the small town like a pack of hungry coyotes.

Jesse stiffened against the sudden tightening in his chest. He hadn't been out here in a long, long time.

Try never.

No, the closest Jesse came was the rodeo arena that sat ten miles outside the city limits.

But this was it. His last trip to the town itself. He was moving on, settling down, living his dream, and that meant laying the past to rest once and for all.

"Sell it," he'd told his lawyer just yesterday.

The mountain of paperwork would be ready for Jesse's signature by the end of the week, which meant he had all of five days to go through what was left of the garage and the old car and salvage anything he might want to keep.

Of course, he'd have to get out of his truck first.

He would.

He was sure there was nothing of value left to keep. Vandals had made off with nearly everything. Old tools. Car parts. After so many years, there wasn't a single thing left.

Still, he'd promised Mr. Lambert he would do a walk-through, and that was what he intended to do.

Tomorrow.

He eyed the car and a memory pushed its way into his head. Of him and his three brothers sleeping on the backseat so many nights when his dad had been too drunk and too volatile for them to be in the house. That had been before the fire, before Pete Gunner had taken them under his wing.

They would have wound up in foster care if it hadn't been for Pete. They should have, but he'd stepped up and fought for them. Eli, too. It had taken three weeks for Pete to win custody. A speedy process compared to the red tape nowadays. But Pete had had money and fame on his side, and a decent lawyer. That, and the county had been underfunded and severely understaffed. They hadn't had the resources to worry over three more children.

Still, the threat of foster care had been real for those few weeks and so Jesse had taken his brothers and gone into hiding in the woods. They'd stayed at an old hunting camp until Pete had finally found them and taken them home.

A real home.

But that first night right after the fire, they'd had only the Buick.

He could still feel the cold upholstery seeping through his clothes, the frustration gripping his insides because he hadn't known what to do or where to go. The fear.

For his younger brothers.

Jesse hadn't given a shit about himself. His future. His life. He'd been angry with the world for dealing him such a shitty hand and so he'd spent his young life pushing fate to the limit. Backing her into a corner and daring her to lash out at him. He'd raced his beat-up motorcycle down Main Street every Saturday night and thumbed his nose at authority and climbed onto any and every bull he could find, to hell with rules and buzzers.

Then.

But there was nothing like a severe concussion and thirteen broken bones to make a guy realize that he actually cared if he lived or died. He'd turned his back on his wild and reckless ways and started taking his career seriously after the Diamond Dust incident. He'd trained smarter, harder, and it had paid off.

He'd finally made it to the top.

Even more, he'd made it out of Lost Gun. The purse he'd won at nationals had been more than enough for a down payment on the Austin spread. And the endorsements that came with being a PBR champion gave him an ongoing income that far surpassed his winnings. For the first time in his life, he was financially set.

And so were his brothers.

Billy and Cole were making their own way on the rodeo circuit, pocketing not only their winnings but endorsements, as well. They were the new faces of rodeo. Young. Good-looking. Lucrative.

A far cry from the scared snot-nosed kids they'd been way back when.

He eyed the dismal landscape one last time. It was time to let go. To move forward and stop looking back.

To move, period.

He'd just keyed the engine and revved the motor when he saw the flash of headlights in his rearview mirror. Gravel crunched as a black BMW pulled up behind him.

A car door opened and slammed shut. Heels crunched toward him. The sweet smell of cupcakes drifted through the open window and Jesse's heartbeat kicked up a notch.

He killed the engine, drew a deep breath and climbed out from behind the wheel.

Yep, it was her, all right. Up close and in person. Three times in the same friggin' day.

So much for keeping his distance.

His groin tightened and he stiffened. "Stalk much?" he asked when Gracie walked up to him.

Her carefully arched brows drew together. "I seem to recall, you were the one who snuck up on me outside the bakery. Besides, I'm not here for you. I'm just keeping an eye on things."

He spared a glance at the falling-down stretch of property. "Not much to see."

"Maybe not yet, but with Tuesday looming and the interest picking up, that's sure to change. Besides, it's right on my way home."

"Still living on Carpenter Street?"

She nodded. "Aunt Cheryl and Uncle E.J. bought a place down in Port Aransas and left the house to me and Charlie."

"How's she doing?"

A smile touched her lips and a softness edged her

gaze. "She's in her second year at the University of Texas. She lives on campus, but she drives home on most weekends. Straight As. Beautiful. She's got a ton of boyfriends."

"What about you?"

"I'm too busy for a boyfriend."

Her words stirred a rush of joy followed by a flood of *What the hell are you thinking?* He didn't care if she did or did not have a significant other. He didn't care about her, period.

Ah, but he still wanted her.

There was no denying the heat that rippled through his body or the crazy way his palms tickled, eager to reach out and see if her skin felt as soft as he remembered.

"Running this city is a full-time job," she went on, "especially with the extra notoriety from *Famous Texas Outlaws.* In addition to the out-of-towners coming in to dig for treasure, Sheriff Hooker caught Myrtle Nell's grandsons trying to drive a forklift over the back fence of this place."

"There is no treasure."

"Which makes it all the more aggravating." Her finger hooked a strand of blond hair that had come loose from her ponytail and she tucked it behind the delicate shell of her ear. "At least if there *was* something left, someone would have already dug it up. The press would have broadcast it from here to kingdom come and all the fuss would have died down. Instead, the D.A. is gearing up for a mess of two-bit trespassing charges."

He wasn't going to touch her. That was what he told himself when the silky tendril of hair came loose again and dangled next to her cheek. No reaching out and sweeping the soft strands away from her face. *No.* "Speaking of charges—" he cleared his suddenly dry throat "—shouldn't Sheriff Hooker be the one keeping an eye on things?"

"He had an anniversary dinner with the missus. I had the time, so I figured I might as well do a quick drive-by." She shrugged. "What about you? What are you doing out here?"

"Just looking around." He forced his gaze away from her and studied his surroundings. His gut tightened.

"I wasn't here when it happened," he heard himself say. A crazy thing to say, but it was so quiet that he almost felt as if he were talking to himself. Except that he could hear her soft even breaths and feel the warmth of her body so close.

But not close enough.

"I was over at the rodeo arena helping out with the horses," he went on, the words slipping through the darkness. "Eli used to pay me to rake the stalls. It was enough to buy lunch for me and my brothers, but sometimes it put me home late. The fire was in full force by the time I got here."

"Where were your brothers that night?"

"They were at the rodeo arena with me. They used to hang out until I finished work so that we could go home together. Eli would let them do their homework in the office. He had a few toys in there, too. To keep them busy while I finished up my chores. Eli dropped us off just up the street that night so my dad wouldn't see him. Silas got mean when he drank and he was always itching for a fight. Not that night, though. We saw the blaze clear down the street. We just didn't know what was burning until we got here."

He could still feel the heat licking at his face long after he'd gone in to discover his father passed out on the couch. Immobile. Unmovable. He'd stood outside afterward, his brothers whimpering beside him. There had been no sound from inside. Just the crackle of flames and the popping of wood.

Because his dad had been dead by then.

That was what Jesse told himself. What he wanted so desperately to believe. Because he didn't want to think he'd left the man in there to die.

"It wasn't your fault," she said, concern edging her words.

As if he didn't know that. He did. He *knew*.

So why the hell did he think that maybe, just maybe, he could have done something more? That he would have? It wasn't as if he hadn't tried. He'd rushed in, his shirt covering his mouth and nose. He'd tugged at the man's lifeless body. He'd begged him to get up. He'd even prayed.

But Silas hadn't budged.

The smoke had gotten thicker and Jesse had had no choice but to retreat. To leave him.

So?

His father had been a selfish SOB and Jesse and his brothers had done a hell of a lot better after he'd passed on. No, Jesse wouldn't have done a damned thing to change that night. He wouldn't have stayed a second longer to try to get him out. He couldn't have stayed.

"It's not going to work," he blurted, eager to change the subject. His gaze slid from her face to her modest blouse and plain navy skirt. The getup wasn't the least bit revealing, but it didn't have to be. The soft material clung to her curves, tracing the voluptuous lines. His dick stirred and he stiffened.

"What are you talking about?"

He motioned to her. "The provocative clothing."

"You think this is provocative?" She glanced down. Her brows knitted with concern as her gaze swiveled back to him. "Did you see a doctor today? Because you took a really hard fall earlier—"

"I'm fine," he cut in, determined to ignore the warmth slip-sliding through him. The last thing he wanted was her concern.

No, he wanted something a lot more basic from Gracie Stone.

And that was the problem in a nutshell. He still wanted her. A desire that neither time nor distance had managed to kill.

Because he'd never had the chance to work her out of his system. To grow tired and bored. Rather, she'd given him a taste of something wonderful, and then she'd taken it away before he'd managed to sate his hunger.

Once he did, he would be done with her like every other woman he'd ever been with. Like the cherries. The first few bites had been heaven, but then he'd gotten really sick, really fast.

And although Jesse Chisholm had no intention of letting his emotions get involved where Gracie Stone was concerned, there suddenly seemed nothing wrong with a little physical contact.

One really hot night with her would be enough to give him some closure. At least that was what he was telling himself.

"I really think you should see a doctor." She eyed him. "Maybe you hit your head."

A grin tugged at his mouth and he couldn't help himself. "Darlin', it's not my head that's aching like a sonofabitch." He closed the distance between them. "At least not the one on my shoulders."

And then he kissed her.

7

HE WAS *KISSING* HER.

Here. Now.

Oh, boy.

His strong, purposeful mouth moved over hers. His tongue swept her bottom lip, licking and nibbling and coaxing and—

Earth to Gracie! This shouldn't be happening. Not here. Not with him. Especially not him.

Just as the denial registered in her shocked brain, he deepened the kiss. His tongue pushed inside, to tease and taunt and tangle with hers. All rational thought faded into a whirlwind of hunger that swirled through her, stirring every nerve. It had been so long since she'd kissed anyone. Since she'd kissed him.

She trembled and her stomach hollowed out.

He tasted even better than the most decadent brownie. Sweeter. Richer. More potent. More addictive.

Before she could stop herself, she leaned into him, melting from the sudden rise in body temperature. Her hand slid up his chest and her fingers caught the soft hair at the nape of his neck.

His arms closed around her. Strong hands pressed against the base of her spine, drawing her closer. She met him chest for chest, hip for hip, until she felt every incredible inch of him flush against her body—the hard planes of his chest, the solid muscles of his thighs, the growing erection beneath his zipper.

Uh-oh.

The warning sounded in her head, but damned if it didn't make her that much more excited. Heat spread from her cheeks, creeping south. The slow burn traveled inch by sweet, tantalizing inch until her nipples throbbed and wetness flooded between her thighs.

And all because of a kiss.

Because the man doing the kissing was wild and careless and completely inappropriate. He was all wrong for her, and damned if she didn't want him in spite of it.

Because of it.

Because Gracie Stone wasn't nearly the goody-goody she pretended to be.

The thought struck and she stiffened. Tearing her lips away, she stumbled backward.

Breathe, she told herself. *Just calm down and breathe.* She couldn't do this. She had responsibilities. "I… You…" She shook her head and tried to ignore the way her lips tingled. "You and I…" She shook her head. "We don't even like each other."

"True enough." He said the words, but the strange flicker in his gaze didn't mirror the sentiment. "But it's not about *like,* sugar. It's about *want.* I want you and you want me. The pull between us…" His gaze darkened as it touched her mouth and she felt the overwhelming chemistry that pulsed between them. "It's strong."

"I should get going," she went on, desperate to kill the tiny hope that he would pull her close and kiss her again.

Lust.

That was all this was.

That and deprivation.

Character, she reminded herself. Deprivation built character. It made her stronger. More resilient.

It also makes you more likely to blow at the first sign of temptation.

His words echoed and she knew he was right.

This was temptation. *He* was temptation in his faded jeans and fitted Western shirt. He practically dripped with sex appeal. He always had. It only stood to reason that her starving hormones would shift into overdrive with him so near.

Which was why she'd made it her business to steer clear of him all these years.

And why she needed to get as far away from him as possible right now.

She backed up, eager to put a few safe inches of distance between them. "I should—"

"I told you to bring the shovel!"

The frantic whisper carried on the warm evening breeze and killed Gracie's hasty retreat.

Jesse's head jerked around toward the old garage and Gracie's gaze followed in time to see a pair of shadows disappear behind the edge of the old structure.

"Call the sheriff." Jesse leaned in his open window and plucked a flashlight from the glove box.

"Wait—" she started, but he was already halfway

up the driveway. "Jesse! Stop! You shouldn't be doing this. It's dangerous...."

Her words faded as he darted behind the old car sitting in front of the garage and disappeared into the darkness. Her heart pounded for the next few seconds as the night seemed to close in. Panic bolted through her.

She darted for her car and snatched her cell phone off the dash. With frantic fingers, she punched in 911 and gave the information to Maureen over at the sheriff's station.

She said a few choice words, all of them involving a headstrong cowboy who should have exercised at least a little bit of caution. But no, he'd run off into the darkness and now she was here. Waiting and worrying and— *Hell,* no.

She couldn't just stand here. She stuffed the phone into her pocket and stepped forward.

She was halfway around the falling-down garage when she heard the chilling voice directly behind her.

"Hold it right there, lady."

The air stalled in her chest and she became keenly aware of the barrel pressed between her shoulder blades. Her heartbeat lurched forward and her hands trembled.

"Take it easy." She held up her hands. "No reason to get upset. We should all just stay calm—"

"Quiet," came the deep, oddly familiar voice.

She knew that voice, which killed the hunch that this was an outsider lured into Lost Gun by all the hype. Her brain started rifling through memories, desperate to find a face to go with the distinctive Southern drawl that echoed in her ears. "Just keep your mouth shut and no one will get hurt. I swear it."

I do solemnly swear to uphold the rules of the Lost Gun Ranger Scouts...

The past echoed, rousing a memory of the Ranger Scouts initiation she'd attended on behalf of the city council.

Her brain started fitting the puzzle pieces together and she frowned. "Troy Warren?" Troy was now a fifteen-year-old sophomore at Lost Gun High and a frequent visitor to the sheriff's office, most memorably after spray-painting I Love Sheila Kimber on the back fence of the middle school. "Is that you?"

"Heck, no," came the voice, slightly frazzled this time. "Ain't nobody here by the name of Warren."

"I know it's you." Gracie summoned her most intimidating voice. "I was standing right behind you at the seventh-grade Scout ceremony." She couldn't help but wonder how a once-upon-a-time Scout ended up with a gun in his hands.

The same way a thirteen-year-old ended up being a provider for his two younger brothers. It was rotten luck. A crazy twist of fate. An accident.

Jesse's image rushed into her head and a wave of panic rolled through her. What if this boy had already shot him?

Even as the possibility rolled through her head, she fought it back down. She would have heard a gunshot. A struggle. *Something.* Anything besides the eerie quiet.

"I told you this was a bad idea," came a second voice. Same slow drawl. Same familiar tone. "She knows your name. She knows your friggin' *name.*"

"She does now," Troy growled to his partner. "You were supposed to keep your mouth shut."

"And let you get us locked up and sent all the way to Huntsville? I knew we shouldn't have come here. I *knew* it."

Gracie's memory stirred again. Same Scout meeting. Different boy. "Lonnie? Lonnie Sawyer? Is that you?"

"No, it ain't him," Troy said. "It's somebody you don't know. A stranger. You just shut up if you know what's good for you—" the barrel nudged between her shoulder blades "—or else."

"Or else what?" The words were out before she could stop them. As scared as she was, she was also getting a little angry. She was sick and tired of having circumstances dictated to her. Of being told what to do and when to do it. Of being stuck. And although she couldn't stand up to the world and change the path of her life, she could change this moment. "You really think you have what it takes to pull the trigger?"

"Heck, yeah."

"Heck, no."

The answers echoed simultaneously and Gracie realized that the three of them had company.

"He's not shooting anybody." Gracie heard Jesse's deep, familiar voice a split second before she heard a grunt and a yelp, and suddenly the gun fell away.

She whirled in time to see Jesse standing between the two teenage boys, hands gripping the backs of their collars. The gun lay forgotten on the ground.

Leaning down, she picked up the discarded weapon and her lips pulled into a frown.

"It's just a paintball gun, Miss Gracie," Lonnie

blurted as she inspected the weapon. "Please don't tell my grandma. *Please*."

"Troy Eugene Warren." She turned on the first boy. "You almost gave me a heart attack." She dangled the weapon. "I thought this was an actual gun."

"It *is* a gun." His stubborn gaze met hers. "It can even break the skin."

"Makes a nasty bruise, too," Lonnie offered. "I know 'cause Troy tested it out on me—"

"What are you boys doing out here?" Jesse cut in, giving them a little shake.

"We're after the money."

"There is no money."

"Says you." Lonnie tried to pull away, but Jesse tightened his grip and held the boy close. "The TV says different," Lonnie blurted. "There's sure to be people coming from as far away as Houston looking for that money. Might as well be somebody right here in town who finds it."

"The money was destroyed in the fire," Gracie said.

"Maybe. But maybe Silas Chisholm just did a damn fine job of hiding it."

"Silas Chisholm wasn't that smart," Jesse growled. "There is no money."

"But—"

"If I catch you trespassing out here again, I'll press charges."

"We're only kids." Troy tried to shrink away. "The cops won't do anything but call our parents."

"Maybe," Gracie added. "But maybe the D.A. will be so outraged when I tell her that you led me to believe you were holding a real gun on me that she'll want to try you both as adults."

"They don't do that."

"Heard it happened over in Magnolia just last week," Jesse offered. "You boys should get at least five to ten for armed assault of a city official."

"Five to ten *years?*" Lonnie looked ready to throw up.

"At the very least," Jesse added. "But I'd bet on an even stiffer sentence since there's an eyewitness—yours truly—who saw you threaten the mayor and hold a gun on her."

"I'm not actually the mayor." The words were out before Gracie could stop them. "I mean, I practically am, but it's not official. Not yet."

Jesse gave her a "too much info" look. "She won by a landslide," Jesse growled in Troy's ear. "She's practically the mayor and you boys are both screwed."

"Please, Mr. Chisholm," Lonnie pleaded. "I can't go to prison. My grandma Lou will kill me."

"I know your grandma. She's a sweet lady. What about you?" Jesse eyed Troy. "How do you think your folks will react?"

"They won't." Troy shrugged. "My daddy don't give a shit. He's drunk most of the time since my ma died."

Gracie didn't miss the strange glimmer in Jesse's eyes before his expression hardened into an unreadable mask. He loosened his grip on both boys. "Go. Get on home. Both of you."

Lonnie's eyes widened. "You're letting us off?"

"Hardly." He pointed a finger. "I want you both at the rodeo arena first thing after school tomorrow."

"For what?"

"To work off the cost of repairing that fence you

just cut." Jesse motioned to his left at the barbed wire that hung open.

"Yes, sir," Lonnie said, snatching up the discarded shovel that lay nearby. "I'll be there. We both will. Ain't that right, Troy?"

"What if we don't show?" Troy eyed Jesse as if trying to gauge just what he could get away with.

"Then I'll file an official complaint with the sheriff and he'll arrest you." Sirens stirred in the background and Gracie knew that Deputy Walker was on his way. Both boys stiffened.

"Come on, Troy," Lonnie pressed. "Just take the deal. Please."

"Okay," Troy grumbled. "But I ain't picking up no horse crap."

"Of course you're not." Jesse grinned. "We don't pick it up. We use a shovel." His expression faded into one of serious intent. "And trust me, I've got plenty of shovels." Troy stiffened and Gracie didn't miss the grin that played at Jesse's lips. She watched as he forced a frown and glanced from one boy to the other. "Now get lost before I change my mind."

The two boys scattered toward the cut fence and disappeared on the other side just as a beige squad car pulled up to the curb.

"Are you okay?" Jesse's gaze collided with hers and if she hadn't known better, she would have sworn she saw concern.

But this was Jesse James Chisholm. Wild. Reckless. Carefree. He didn't give a shit about anyone. That was why she'd been so drawn to him all those years ago. He'd been a kindred spirit. Just as wild as she'd been. As reckless. As carefree.

If only she could remember that when he looked at her.

"That was a really nice thing you did," she told him. "Giving those boys a chance."

"Shoveling isn't a chance. It's hard work. Trust me, they'll be begging for me to file charges before I'm through with them." That was what he said, but she didn't miss the softness in his eyes. While he played the same "I don't give a shit" Jesse he'd been way back when, something had changed. He'd changed.

Even if he didn't seem as if he wanted to admit it.

A rush of warmth went through her that had nothing to do with the fierce attraction between them and everything to do with the fact that she admired him almost as much as she lusted after him.

Before she could dwell on the unsettling thought, she turned her attention to the deputy who rushed up, gun drawn, gaze scouring the landscape.

"I came as soon as I got the call," he said in between huge gulps of air. "I was right in the middle of Wednesday-night bowling. Just threw a strike." He drank in a few more drafts of air. "So where are they? Where are the perpetrators?"

"False alarm, Dan."

"But I ran two blocks just to get to the squad car on account of mine is in the shop and my wife dropped me off at the bowling alley."

"Sorry."

"But you said we had trespassers. Two of them."

"They turned out to be just a couple of kids taking a shortcut on their way home," Jesse added. "No harm, no foul."

Dan glanced around a few more seconds before

shoving his gun back in his holster. "Doggone it. I shoulda known it was too early for any real excitement. That TV show doesn't air until next week. It'll be the usual snoozefest until then."

"Not true. It's bingo night at the Ladies' Auxiliary tomorrow night. That should mean at least three cat-fights and maybe even an incarceration," Gracie reminded him.

"Stop trying to cheer me up. You need a ride home?"

"I've got my car but thanks."

"You folks take care, then." The deputy turned. "If I hurry, I should be able to get back before the game is over. Not that I'll win now, on account of I missed my turn...."

"So?" Jesse eyed her when Dan walked away. His gaze darkened and the temperature seemed to kick up a few degrees.

Every nerve in her body went on high alert because she knew something was about to happen between them. She knew and she couldn't make herself walk away. "So what?" she managed, her lips trembling.

"Are you going to finish what you started with that kiss or not?"

8

"I DISTINCTLY REMEMBER *you* kissed *me*."

A grin tugged at his lips, but the expression didn't quite touch the depths of his eyes, which were a deep, mesmerizing violet. "Then are you going to finish what I started?"

Yes. No. Maybe.

The answers raced through her mind and her heartbeat kicked up a notch. "I don't know what you mean," she said, despite the fact that she knew. She knew because she knew him. The wicked gleam in his eyes. The heat rolling off his body.

Even more, she knew herself. The bad girl buried deep inside who urged her to take the initiative and make the first move. And the second. And the third.

She swallowed against the sudden lump in her throat and tried to get a grip. "I think you're misreading the situation."

"You want me and I want you." He stared deep into her eyes. "We should do something about it."

"Not happening," she blurted, despite the *yeah, baby* echoing through her. "I'm the mayor."

"Soon-to-be mayor."

"I can't just go around hopping into bed with every cowboy who propositions me. I mean, yes, I liked the kiss, but that's beside the point. We're all wrong for each other."

"You say that like it matters."

"It does."

Pure sin teased the corner of his sensual lips. "I don't want to date you, Gracie." His gaze collided with hers. "I want to have sex with you."

She wasn't sure why his words sent a wave of disappointment through her. It wasn't as if she *wanted* to date him. Sure, he'd changed from the wild, careless boy he'd once been, but he was still Jesse James Chisholm. Still off-limits. Still temporary.

And Gracie had sworn off temporary when she'd turned her life around.

"It's obvious there's something between us," he murmured, his deep voice vibrating along her nerve endings. "Something fierce."

"I think—"

"That's the problem," he cut in. "You do too much thinking. You ought to start feeling again. You might like it."

Before she could respond, he pressed a key card into her hand, kissed her roughly on the lips and walked to his truck.

The engine grumbled, the taillights flashed and just like that, he was gone.

She stared at the plastic card burning into her hand. The Lost Gun Motel. It was the only one in town. Right on Main Street, next to the diner, the parking lot in full view of anyone who happened by.

Not that she was thinking about taking him up on his offer. Having sex with Jesse Chisholm would be the worst idea ever.

Because?

Because they were polar opposites. He was wild and exciting and she wasn't. At least she was doing her damnedest to prove that she wasn't.

And that was the problem in a nutshell. Jesse called to the bad girl inside of her. He made her want to forget the past twelve years of walking the straight and narrow. Forget the pain of losing her brother. Forget the promise she'd made to Charlie.

To herself.

Not happening. She had an image to uphold. A reputation to protect. She was the mayor, for heaven's sake.

Sort of.

She hadn't actually taken the oath.

Anxiety rushed through her as she climbed into her car and started for home. As committed as she was to the path she'd chosen, she couldn't help but feel as if she'd missed out on something.

On life.

On lust.

Forget the slutty college years. She'd spent hers taking extra classes at the university so that she could graduate early and earn an apprenticeship with the city planner's office. She'd missed out on so much. That was why she was feeling so much anxiety about the upcoming inauguration. Once she took her oath, her life would be set, the commitment made, her chance lost.

She wanted one more night with Jesse. One more memory. Then she could stop fantasizing and go back to her nice conservative life and step up as the town's new mayor without any worries or regrets.

She *would*.

But not just yet.

She slammed on the brakes, swung the car around and headed for the motel.

"Okay," she blurted ten minutes later when Jesse opened the motel door to find her standing on his doorstep. "Let's do it."

And then *she* reached out and kissed *him*.

THE MOMENT GRACIE touched her lips to his, Jesse felt a wave of heat roll through him. The real thing was even better than he remembered. She felt warmer. Smelled sweeter. Tasted even more decadent.

Her tongue tangled with his and she slid her arms around his neck. Her small fingers played in his hair. Heat shimmered down his spine from the point of contact.

His gut tightened and his body throbbed. He steered her around, backed her up into the hotel room and kicked the door shut with his boot. Pulling her blouse free of her skirt, he shoved his hands beneath the soft material. She was warm and soft and oh so addictive against the rough pads of his fingertips. His body trembled with need and he urged her toward the bed.

He shoved aside the duffel bag sitting on top and guided her down. He pulled back, his hands going to the button on his jeans. He made quick work of them, shoving the denim down his legs so fast that it was a wonder he didn't fall and bust his ass. He'd spent so many nights fantasizing about her and now she was real.

Warm.

Soft.

A passing spray of headlights spilled through the windows and she seemed to stiffen. As if she feared someone would bust through the door any moment and see them together. Because as much as she wanted him, she still had her doubts. Her fears.

Jesse fought for his control and steeled himself against the delicious heat coming off her body. He could wipe away the doubt if he wanted to. All he had to do was speed up and push things along as fast and as furious as the heat that zipped up and down his spine. She would be so mindless that she wouldn't care if they were standing on the fifty-yard line of the local football stadium at half-time.

But he didn't want her mindless. He wanted her on the offensive. He wanted her to want this despite the consequences.

He wanted her to want him with the same passion she'd felt so long ago.

That meant slowing down and giving her the chance to think about what was happening, to feel each and every moment, to forget her fear and give in to the heat that raged between them.

He closed his hands over her shoulders and steered her down onto the mattress. His fingers caressed the soft material of her blouse, molding the silk to her full breasts.

Easy, slick. Just take it easy.

The warning echoed in his head and he managed to move his hands away before he could stroke her perfectly outlined nipples.

He would. But not just yet.

He scooted down to pull off her heels and toss them

to the floor. One hand lingered at her ankle and he couldn't help himself. He traced the curve of her calf up to her knee and smiled as he heard her breath catch. Then his fingers went to the button on her skirt. His heart pounded and his pulse raced and an ache gripped him from the inside out. He stiffened, fighting the lust that roared inside of him.

Easy...

He grabbed the waistband and helped her ease the navy material down her hips, her legs, revealing a pair of black lace panties that betrayed the prim-and-proper image she fought so hard to maintain.

He knew then that there was still a little of the old Gracie deep inside and his heartbeat kicked up a notch.

His fingertips brushed her bare skin, grazing and stirring the length of her legs as he worked the skirt free. The friction ripped through him, testing his control with each delicious inch.

Finally he reached her ankles. He stood near the foot of the bed and pulled the skirt completely off.

His gaze traveled from her calves up her lush thighs to the wispy lace barely covering the soft strip of silk between her legs. He grew harder, hotter, and anticipation zipped up and down his spine.

He swallowed, his mouth suddenly dry. With a sweep of his tongue he licked his lips. The urge to feel her pressed against his mouth nearly sent him over the edge. He wanted to part her with his tongue and taste her sweetness.

Need pounded, steady and demanding through his body, and sent the blood jolting through his veins at an alarming rate.

He dropped to the bed beside her and reached out.

His fingers brushed the velvet of one hip and that was all it took. Suddenly his hands seemed to move of their own accord, skimming the length of her body to explore every curve, every dip. He lingered at the lace covering her moist heat and traced the pattern with his fingertip. He moved lower, feeling the pouty slit between her legs.

She gasped and her legs fell open.

He followed the scrap of lace, his fingertip brushing the sensitive flesh on either side. The urge to dip his finger beneath the scant covering and plunge deep into her lush body almost undid him.

Almost.

But he wouldn't.

Because it wasn't about what he wanted. It was all about her at that particular moment. About convincing her that this was right. That *he* was right.

About making sure that this moment exceeded her expectations and made it impossible for her to turn her back on him again.

Jesse forced his hand up over her flat belly. Her soft flesh quivered beneath his palm as he moved higher, pushing her blouse aside until he uncovered one creamy breast.

His fingertips circled the rose-colored nipple, and he inhaled sharply when the already turgid peak ripened ever more. Leaning over, he touched his lips to her navel, dipped his tongue inside and swirled. She whimpered, the sound urging him on. He licked a path up her fragrant skin, teased and nibbled, until he reached one full breast. He drew the swollen tip deep into his mouth and suckled her.

He swept his hands downward, cupping her heat

through the scanty V of her panties. Wisps of silky hair brushed his palm like licks of fire and his groin throbbed.

She gasped and then it was as if the floodgates opened. She grabbed his hand and guided him closer. Her pelvis lifted, coming up off the bed, searching, begging for his touch.

The sound of a car door outside pushed past the frantic beat of his heart and he noted the flash of headlights that spilled around the edges of the blinds.

"The door's unlocked," he pointed out.

"So?" she breathed and he knew she was beyond caring at the moment.

Satisfaction rolled through him, followed by a punch of lust as he slid a finger deep inside her warm, sweet body. And then he started to pleasure her.

9

GRACIE STARED UP at the man looming over her. His finger plunged deep and she closed her eyes for a long moment before he withdrew. Her eyelids fluttered open in time to feel him part her just a fraction before tracing her moist slit. He knew just how to turn her on.

He knew her.

Her heart.

Her soul.

Her.

Hardly.

If he'd been the least bit clued in to the real Gracie Stone, the one who wore sweats and ate healthy snacks and watched late-night reality TV, he would have dropped her just like that. That was who she was now. She was nothing like the wild and wicked girl who'd climbed into the bed of his pickup truck way back when.

Even if she had done something only a bona fide bad girl would do—she'd chased him down and now they were going at it.

Still…he'd been the one to issue the proposition, to make the first move.

She held tight to the notion. But then he pushed a finger deep inside and all thought fled.

She gasped, her lips parting, her eyes drifting closed at the intimate caress.

"Open your eyes," Jesse demanded, his voice raw with lust. "Look at me."

Gracie obeyed and he caught her gaze. He slipped another finger inside her.

Her legs turned to butter. Her knees fell open, giving him better access. But he didn't go deeper and give her more of what she wanted. Instead, he stared down at her, his gaze so compelling that she couldn't help herself. She arched her hips shamelessly, rising up to meet him, drawing him in.

The more she moved, the deeper he went. The pressure built.

"That's it, sugar. Just go with it."

She continued to move from side to side, creating the most delicious friction, her insides slick, sweltering from his invasion. She tried to breathe, to pull oxygen into her lungs, but she couldn't seem to get enough. Pleasure rippled from her head to her toes, and the room seemed to spin around her. Her hips rotated. Her nerves buzzed.

Incredible.

That was what this was.

What *he* was.

Her head fell back. Her lips parted. A low moan rumbled up her throat and spilled past her lips.

He leaned down and caught the sound with his mouth. His hand fell away from her as he thrust his tongue deep, mimicking the careful attention his purposeful fingers had given her only seconds before.

Straddling her, his knees trapped her thighs. He leaned back to gaze down at her.

She touched his bare chest, felt the wisps of dark silky hair beneath her palm, the ripple of hard, lean muscle as he sucked in a deep breath. Her attention shifted lower and she grasped him, trailing her hand up and down his hard, throbbing shaft. His flesh pulsed in her palm and a shiver danced up her spine. She wanted to feel him. She wanted it more than she'd ever wanted anything.

He thrust into her grip as she worked him for several long moments before he caught her wrist and forced her hand away.

And then he touched her.

His hands started on her rib cage, sliding over her skin, learning every nuance. He touched her anywhere, everywhere, as if he couldn't get enough of her. As if he wanted to burn the memory of her into his head because he knew they would have only this one night.

That was it. She knew it and so did he.

If only the truth didn't bother her so much.

Before she could dwell on that fact, he lowered his head and drew her nipple into the moist heat of his mouth. Suddenly the only thing on her mind was touching him. She slid her hands over his shoulders, feeling his warm skin and hard muscle, memorizing every bulge, every ripple.

He suckled her breast, his teeth grazing the soft skin, nipping and biting with just enough pressure to make her gasp. Her breast swelled and throbbed.

Jesse licked a path across her skin to coax the other

breast in the same torturous manner. A decadent heat spiraled through her and she rubbed her pelvis against him.

"Please." She wanted him, surrounding her, inside of her.

"Not yet," he murmured. He slid down her slick body and left a blazing path with the teasing tip of his tongue. Strong, purposeful hands parted her thighs. Almost reverently, he stroked her quivering sex. "I've thought about doing this so many times. I never had the chance that first night."

Their only night.

They'd both been so crazy with excitement that it had been fast and furious, and pretty fantastic.

But this… This went way beyond that night.

The breath rushed from her lungs when she felt his damp mouth against the inside of one thigh. Then his lips danced across her skin to the part of her that burned the fiercest.

She gasped as his tongue parted her. He eased his hands under her buttocks, tilting her to fit more firmly against his mouth. His shoulders urged her legs apart until she lay completely open. He nuzzled her, drinking in her scent before he devoured her with his mouth. Every thrust of his tongue, every caress of his lips, felt like a raw act of possession. Complete. Powerful.

Mine.

As soon as the thought pushed its way into her head, she pushed it right back out. There was no hidden meaning behind his actions. It was all about pleasure. About instant gratification. Sex.

His fingers parted her slick folds and his tongue swept her. Up and down. Back and forth. This way and that.

Heat drenched her. She bucked and her body convulsed. A rush of moisture flooded between her thighs, and he lapped at her as if he'd never tasted anything so sweet.

When she calmed to a slight shudder, he left her on the bed to rummage in his pocket for a condom. A few seconds later he slid the latex down his rigid penis and followed her down onto the mattress. Pulling her close, he kissed her long and slow and deep. She tasted her own essence—wild and ripe, bitter and sweet—on his lips. Desire spurted through her. Her blood pounded. Her insides tensed and she clutched at his shoulders.

He wedged a thigh between her legs and positioned himself. Thrusting, he joined them in one swift complete motion. The air rushed from her lungs and she gasped.

He pulsed deep inside of her for a long decadent moment before he started to move. He withdrew, only to push back inside, burying himself deep.

Over and over and over.

She skimmed her hands along his back, wanting him harder and faster, racing toward the bubbling heat of another climax. She clutched at his shoulders. She cried out his name.

He buried himself one last time deep in her body and went rigid. A groan rumbled from his throat as he gave in to his own release. He stiffened, bucking once, twice, before collapsing atop her. He nuzzled her neck, his lips warm against her frantic pulse beat.

She cupped his cheek and felt the roughness of his skin. The faint hint of stubble tickled her palm and she had the sudden thought that this—this closeness—felt almost as good as everything leading up to it.

The notion sent a rush of panic through her because tonight wasn't about getting close to Jesse. She'd had that once before and it had been even more addictive than the most decadent brownie. No, this was all about sex. About hooking up with him this one last time and building another sweet memory to add to her store before she took the oath and said goodbye to her past once and for all.

Mission accomplished.

She barely resisted the urge to wrap her arms around his neck and kiss him again. Instead, she slid out from under him and started snatching up her clothes.

He leaned up on one elbow and eyed her. "What the hell are you doing?"

"Leaving. I need to be up early in the morning. Really early."

"Gracie—"

"That was nice." Nice? "I mean, great. Really great. Thanks," she blurted for lack of anything better to say.

And then she headed for the door before she gave in to the wild woman inside who urged her to turn around and jump his bones again.

And again.

And *again*.

She wanted to. She wanted it so bad that it scared her and so she moved faster, shrugging on her skirt and blouse in record time and stepping into her shoes.

It wasn't until she heard the voices from the walkway outside that she slowed down. Her hand stalled on the doorknob.

"This has to be the room. The maid said so."

"Knock, then, and we'll find out."

The wood rattled against her grip and Gracie

jumped. Jesse was on his feet in that next instant. He peered past the edge of the drapes, a tight expression etching his face.

"Who is it?" Her voice was a breathless whisper.

"A couple of guys I've never seen before," he told her. "One of them has a camera."

"Reporters," she murmured. "Trina said there were a few checking in today." Her gaze locked with his. "What am I going to do?"

A dark look carved his face for a long moment, but then his expression softened. "Wait a sec." He grabbed his jeans and pulled them on just as another knock sounded. A third knock and he reached for the doorknob. "I'll distract them and you can slip out." He pressed his lips roughly to hers, urged her back behind the door and then hauled it open.

"What the hell, dude?" He glared at the two men before stepping outside. "I'm trying to sleep." The door closed behind him.

"We just have a few questions—"

"That you can damned well ask at a decent hour. I'm filing a complaint with management."

She peeked past the edge of the drapes in time to see Jesse start down the walkway and disappear inside the motel lobby a few doors down. The reporters trailed after him, snapping a few pictures along the way. In a matter of seconds, they'd piled inside after him, their attention fixated on Silas Chisholm's oldest son, and the coast was clear.

Gracie drew a deep, calming breath, but it didn't help. Her heart still pounded, her blood rushed and her nerves buzzed, and none of it had anything to do with the fact that she'd almost been caught red-handed by the press. She was worked up because, despite the damage it might do to her reputation, she wanted to rip off her clothes and hop back into bed to wait for another round of hot, mind-blowing sex.

Jesse was dangerous to her peace of mind because he made her forget all about what she *should* do and reminded her of what she *wanted* to do.

Of the girl she'd been so long ago and how she'd lusted after him with a passion she hadn't felt in the twelve years since.

A passion she would never feel again after tonight.

She ignored the depressing thought and held tight to the fact that she'd yet to start her acceptance speech and she still needed to come up with a strategy to get past Big Earl's dogs.

She drew a deep breath, pulled open the door and did a quick check to make sure the coast was still clear. And then she made a beeline for her car parked several spaces down.

Climbing behind the wheel, she gave one last look at the main lobby, hoping to catch a glimpse of Jesse through the glass doors. Instead, she saw Hazel Trevino, the motel's manager, gesturing wildly while on the phone and she knew the woman was calling the police to report the disruptive reporters.

Which meant Deputy Walker would be responding any second and the last thing Gracie needed was to be seen sitting outside the local motel, her hair mussed, her lips swollen, her cheeks pink.

Talk about fuel for gossip.

She fought down a wave of regret, shoved the key into the ignition and headed home.

"Show's over, folks." Deputy Walker waved a hand at the small crowd gathered in front of the check-in desk in the motel lobby. "You two, get out." He motioned to the reporters.

"But we're staying here."

"Then get back to your rooms and leave everyone alone."

"But we just have a few questions—"

"Which you'll be asking from jail if you don't get going right now." Deputy Walker pulled open the door and motioned the two men outside. "I'll see you back to your rooms myself."

"Sorry about that, Mr. Chisholm." Hazel Trevino was in her late forties with black eyes to match her dark hair. "Hope you won't hold the disturbance against us. We usually run a nice quiet place here. But with all the hoopla about this whole *Famous Texas Outlaws* episode, I guess it's to be expected."

"It's not your fault."

"It's not yours, either." Hazel smiled. "I know how folks treat you around here, but you ain't your pa. Some of us are smart enough to know that."

"Thanks, Miss Hazel."

"None necessary. You'd think folks could just let sleeping dogs lie."

"Not when they think money is involved."

Her eyes took on an eager light. "You really think all that money went up in flames?"

Jesse shrugged. "If not, someone would have surely found it by now."

"Probably. We had more than our share of treasure hunters the first time it aired. Why, I remember watching it on TV. Wilbur and I had just got married. Even thought about looking for the cash ourselves. Would have made a nice little nest egg to raise our boys, but then his daddy passed and left us this place and just like that, we had our hands full."

"It's a nice place."

"Lord knows we try to run a tight ship." She reached into a drawer. "I hope you won't let tonight spoil your visit. Here's a free voucher for the Rusty Pig. Your next plate of barbecue ribs is on us."

He nodded at the motel manager and headed back to his room. A wave of disappointment swept through him when he walked inside to find the room empty. Not that he'd expected Gracie to wait for him. The whole point of throwing himself to the wolves had been to give her a chance to escape.

Still, a part of him had held out a tiny sliver of hope. The part of him that had longed to fit in all those years ago. To belong to a town that had never given him the time of day, to befriend the very people who'd turned their backs on him.

Which was most people.

There were a few, like Pete and Hazel, who'd refused to hold him accountable for someone else's sins. They'd always treated him decent.

But Jesse had wanted more.

He'd wanted to walk into church every Sunday without half the congregation staring at him as if he'd forgotten to wipe his boots. He'd wanted to walk down Main Street without people whispering behind his back. He'd wanted to spread out a blanket at the town picnic and share a slice of apple pie with Gracie Stone in front of God and the Ladies' Auxiliary.

He'd wanted to fit in.

Like hell. Fitting in was just a pipe dream he'd come to terms with a long, long time ago. He never would and that was okay. *He* was okay. Healthy. Successful. Happy.

He didn't give a shit what anyone thought.

But she did, and damned if that didn't bother him even more than when he'd been the one eager to fit into a town that had long ago locked him out.

He fought down the feelings and debated climbing back into bed and trying for some shut-eye. That was what he would have done after a pretty incredible sexual encounter. What he needed to do right now. He had a busy day tomorrow. He had two more bulls to sell and then he needed to get the rest of his stock shipped off to Austin, and he needed to make plans for the bachelor party.

He didn't need to feel so on edge, his muscles tight, his mind racing. As if he still sat poised at the starting gate rather than at the top of the scoreboard after a wildly successful ride.

Crazy.

The whole point of sleeping with Gracie was to give him some relief. So that he could stop thinking about her. Stop wanting her. Stop fantasizing.

Stop!

He snatched up his keys and his gaze snagged on a scrap of black lace peeking from between the sheets. He leaned down and scooped up the forgotten lingerie. His fingers tightened as a detailed memory of the past few hours washed over him. Her body pressed to his, her hands touching him, her voice whispering through his head, each syllable softened with that honey-sweet drawl that had haunted his dreams too many times to count. She tried so hard to hide her passionate nature, but it was there, bubbling just below the surface, waiting for the chance to fire up and boil over.

She hadn't even come close tonight.

Sure, she'd exploded in his arms, but he couldn't shake the feeling that she'd still been holding back.

Below the surface, she'd still been controlled. Restrained. Caged.

Shoving the undies in his pocket, he grabbed a shirt and his keys. A few minutes later he left the motel behind and headed out to the rodeo arena for the kind of ride that could actually tire him out.

Otherwise it was going to be one hell of a long night.

It was the longest night of Gracie Stone's life.

She came to that conclusion several hours later as she tossed and turned and tried to forget Jesse and the all-important fact that she'd had *the* best orgasm of her life.

She'd known it would be great. That had been the point of going to his motel room in the first place. To experience a little greatness before she doomed herself to the monotony of small-town politics.

At the same time, she'd sort of secretly hoped that it might be disastrous so that maybe, just maybe, she would want to forget it. Him. The two of them.

Fat chance.

Instead of putting tonight behind her, she kept thinking how great it would be to head back over to the motel and do it again. And again.

Not that she would ever do such a thing. Instead, she was doing anything—everything—to keep her mind off of him and her hands away from the car keys.

She answered email and cleaned out her refrigerator and watched three back-to-back *Bridezillas* reruns on cable and even checked her voice mail. Three messages from Trina detailing tomorrow's schedule and one from her sister.

"I just wanted to give you a heads-up." Charlie's voice carried over the line. "I've got study sessions on Friday and Saturday for my economics test on Monday. So I won't be able to make it down this weekend. Call you later." *Beep.*

"So much for homemade pizzas," she told Sugar Lips, who wagged her tail frantically before racing for the back door. That made four weeks in a row that Charlie hadn't been able to make it home.

Not that Gracie was counting.

In the two years since her sister had gone away to school, she'd seen her less and less. Which was a good thing. It meant Charlie was growing up, becoming independent, relying on herself instead of clinging to Gracie.

At the same time, she couldn't help but feel a little lonely because Charlie was the one making the break, pulling away, getting out of Lost Gun. Meanwhile, Gracie was stuck here. That was the promise she'd made to her sister and she intended to keep it regardless of what direction Charlie took with her life. She wanted her sister to have a home base. A place to come back to when life kicked her a little too hard.

She wanted Charlie to have the home Gracie herself had never had.

She finished listening to one more message from Trina reminding her about a meeting with the local library committee and then headed to the kitchen for a chocolate cupcake.

Okay, so it wasn't a cupcake.

If only she'd had a cupcake or a cookie or a candy bar, then maybe, just maybe, she wouldn't feel so deprived.

Instead, she scarfed a handful of Wheat Thins and then went after a glass of ice water. Her hands trembled as she turned on the faucet and her gaze shifted to Sugar, who sat nearby, her ragged stuffed animal beneath her. The maltipom wrestled for a few seconds with the worn toy before whimpering when she couldn't seem to get it beneath her for a little humping action.

"I know the feeling." She downed half the glass, but it did nothing to ease the heat swamping her from the inside out.

She still felt nervous.

Frazzled.

Disappointed.

She ignored the last thought and took another drink. Disappointed? Because Jesse hadn't come running after her? Begging her for round two?

A one-night stand, she reminded herself. That was all tonight had been. All it could ever be, because Gracie had an image to protect. She was a leader now. A role model.

She'd made a promise to the town.

Just as she'd made a promise to her sister to be there when Charlie needed her.

Even if Charlie didn't seem to need her all that much anymore.

She ditched the thought along with the glass of water

and headed back upstairs. She bypassed the bedroom and headed straight for the bathroom. Since a glass of ice water had failed to cool her down, maybe a cold shower would do the trick.

Hopefully.

Because the last thing, the very last thing, Gracie intended to do was to climb back into her car and head back over to Jesse's motel room.

No matter how much she suddenly wanted to.

10

"I KNEW YOU still had it in you," Trina declared when Gracie walked into City Hall a half hour late the next morning.

After an endless night spent tossing and turning and trying to forget all about Jesse Chisholm. "What are you talking about?"

"You and a certain PBR champion."

"How did you find out?" She had the sudden vision of her and Jesse spread across the front page of *Lost Gun Weekly,* all the important body parts blacked out to preserve the newspaper's reputation.

But still…

She fought down a sliver of excitement and held tight to the fear coiling inside her. "The newspaper?"

"I admit that you gallivanting with anyone is definitely worthy of front-page treatment, but no. Kathy Mulcany heard it from Laura Lou Spencer, who heard it from Mitchell Presley, who said he was just hanging out watching the domino game with the Amberjack twins when he saw you and Jesse in front of Sarah's Sweets."

"The bakery? That's what the 'attagirl' was all about?"

"I'll admit I would rather hear that you were getting a little action instead of talking, but a girl has to start somewhere, I s'pose."

"We weren't talking. I mean, we were, but not in a social capacity. Trespassers," Gracie blurted. "He was worried about trespassers and I told him I would have the sheriff keep an eye on his place."

"So he didn't invite you out?"

"Of course not."

"And you didn't invite him out?"

"No." Technically she'd invited him *in.* A wave of heat swept through her and she cleared her suddenly dry throat. "Are the, um, painters here yet?"

"They're taping up edges right now." She eyed the cupcake sitting on her desk. "Look what the church ladies dropped off. There were six, but I didn't have time for breakfast so I scarfed down a few and gave the receptionist next door some. I guess I'll just save this one for later since you're always on a diet—"

"I'll take it." She snatched the vanilla goody out of Trina's hand.

"Really?"

Yeah, really?

"Picking out paint colors can be taxing work." That and she'd worked up an appetite last night that she'd yet to satisfy, particularly after two pieces of whole wheat toast and a grapefruit for breakfast.

She needed carbs in the worst way.

That or another night with Jesse.

Since option number two was out of the question,

she would have to settle for second best. Besides, it was just one teeny tiny cupcake.

"I'd be happy to get you a bran muffin." Trina eyed her. "I know how you hate to cheat."

"That's okay, I don't mind cheating a little. Besides, maybe they're sugar-free. With whole wheat flour and egg substitute. I heard Myrtle Nell is experimenting with some new Weight Watchers recipes. This is probably the result."

"It's not," Trina said, snatching the cake out of her hand. "Trust me, I've had three. There's nothing weight conscious about it." She set the vanilla confection on the far side of her desk. "I'll get you a bran muffin."

Gracie thought about arguing, but Trina was already looking at her as if she'd grown a third eye. She swallowed against the rising hunger and focused on the stack of papers on the edge of her assistant's desk. "So what's on the agenda for today?" She rifled through the papers. "A city council meeting? A water commission hearing?"

Trina plucked the papers from her hands and returned them to their spot. "The Senior Ladies expect you for their weekly breakfast in the morning, and then there's the middle school car wash. Then there's the Daughters of the Republic of Texas bake sale. It's at three o'clock on Thursday. The local kindergarten is also having their fundraiser on Thursday afternoon. I've also got you scheduled to lead the Pledge of Allegiance at the quilting circle on Friday morning. In the meantime, when you're not playing the goodwill ambassador—" Trina smiled and motioned to the open doorway "—you get to redecorate your new office."

Forget getting out and about today to distract herself. She was going to be cooped up all afternoon in her shell of an office. With nothing but flooring samples and furniture catalogs and her own damnable thoughts. Gracie swallowed again. "Now I *really* need a cupcake."

"YOUR CONCENTRATION'S for shit," Eli told Jesse when he finally managed to catch his breath after taking a nosedive off the back of an ornery bull.

"Stop giving me grief and help me back up, old man." It was early in the afternoon and his fifth time in the dust in as many hours.

Eli held out a hand. "I think you've had your butt beat enough for one day. Yesterday I could understand. You had that pretty young thing to catch your eye. But today?"

Today was worse. Yesterday Gracie had just snagged his eye. Today she was under his skin, in his head.

Why, he couldn't rightly say.

Last night had gone just like any other night with any other woman. They'd gotten down to business and then bam, she'd walked away. No talking or cuddling or sleeping over.

That fact bothered him a helluva lot more than it should have considering he'd gone into last night knowing full well where he stood.

Sex.

That was all he'd been interested in. That was all she'd been interested in.

At the same time, he couldn't forget the way she'd pressed her lips against the side of his throat and hesitated. As if leaving wasn't as easy as she'd thought.

The possibility had eased the throbbing in his shoulders enough so he could close his eyes. Or maybe it had been the swig of whiskey he'd downed the minute he'd walked back into the empty room after causing enough of a distraction for her to slip out unnoticed.

To preserve his own reputation.

That was what he told himself. The last thing he needed was the two of them all over the local paper. The *Weekly* would have them committed and married within a few paragraphs and his image as rodeo's hottest bad boy would be blown to hell and back.

He surely hadn't done it because she'd looked so petrified that he'd wanted—no, *needed*—to do something to ease the fear.

So he'd waltzed out of the room for a run-in with a duo from a local news network out of Austin and given her a way out.

"…if you don't start paying attention, you're going to split your head open."

He ignored the disappointment churning inside him and focused on Eli and the brand-new bull kicking and spitting across the arena.

Shitkicker had been delivered first thing that morning from a breeder out of California. He would have had the bull shipped straight to Austin, but the breeder had been ahead of schedule and so he'd arrived in Lost Gun instead. A descendant of two of the most notorious rodeo bulls to ever buck a rider, Kicker was two thousand pounds of pure whup-ass and had cost him a load of money. Well spent, of course. Jesse hadn't gotten to be the best by training halfway. He went all out in the practice arena, just the way he went all out during any ride.

Because every ride meant something.

Every time he climbed onto the back of a bull, he was one step closer to the next championship.

Another step away from the scared, angry kid he'd been way back when.

He focused on dusting off and heading back to the bull pen, where Troy and Lonnie, the trespassing duo from the night before, were busy shoveling manure. And complaining every step of the way.

"Let me use the shovel and you hold the bucket."

"I'm on shovel duty for at least fifteen minutes. Stop bellyaching and just hold the bucket steady."

Shit plopped over the side and both boys cursed.

Jesse would have smiled, except he didn't feel much like smiling. He drank in a deep draft of hay and manure, but instead of smelling either, he smelled Gracie. The clean scent of her skin. The strawberry sweetness of her hair. The ripe, decadent aroma of her sex.

Gracie had been there for so long in his memories, taunting and teasing and tempting him. One brief encounter wouldn't be nearly enough to get her out of his system. He needed to overindulge, to satisfy himself over and over until he was sick of her. Gracie was like that overflowing basket of cherries. One night with her wouldn't be enough to make him swear off her completely.

He needed more.

A lot more.

He bypassed the boys and pushed open the corral gate.

"Where you going?" Eli called after him.

"I've got business in town."

Eli chuckled. "I'll just bet."

Jesse was going after Gracie Stone, all right, and

they were going to put out this fire that burned between them once and for all.

But first…

First it was going to get hot.

Very hot.

"I CAN HARDLY BREATHE," Gracie told Trina as she stood in the middle of the mess that would soon be her new office. The painters had finished two of the walls, but the rest they'd left until tomorrow. She fanned herself with a circle of paint swatches and eyed her assistant. "Is it hot in here or is it just me?"

"The electrician had to kill the power to the air conditioner unit supplying this room in order to replace the old ducts."

"That explains it."

"That and him." Trina stared past Gracie. "He definitely kicks up the body temp a few degrees."

Gracie turned to see the man who filled her open doorway. Faded jeans clung to his muscular legs. A crisp white T-shirt stretched over his hard, broad chest. Stubble shadowed his strong jaw. Her gaze collided with a pair of violet eyes, as rich and lush as crushed velvet. The air stalled in her lungs.

"If it isn't the infamous Jesse James Chisholm," Trina said. "To what do we owe the honor of this visit?"

"I've got some unfinished business with our new mayor." Jesse closed the distance between them and stopped just scant inches away.

"I'm not the mayor," Gracie heard herself say. "Not yet." Trina gave her a knowing look and she shrugged. "So, um, what can I do for you?"

"Actually, it's about what I can do for you." He

grinned and pulled her black undies from his pocket. The scrap of dark lace dangled from one tanned finger. "You forgot these."

Gracie's heart stopped beating.

Trina cleared her throat. "I, um, really should get going. It's ladies' night over at the saloon and I've got to pick up my dry cleaning and get my eyebrows waxed. I always knew you had it in you," Trina murmured a split second before she hightailed it for the door. "I'll be leaving now. For good. So you'll have plenty of privacy to, um, talk, or whatever." The click of a door punctuated the sentence and then she was gone.

"We've been painting," Gracie blurted, eager to drown out the thunder of her own traitorous heart. "Sahara Tan." She eyed one of the finished walls.

"Tan, huh?" Jesse rubbed the silky material of her underwear between his two fingers in a sensual caress she felt from her head clear to the tips of her toes.

Crazy. He wasn't even close to touching her.

Not now. But last night? He'd touched. And teased. And seduced. And damned if she didn't want him to do it all over again.

Heat uncoiled in her stomach, followed by a slow burning embarrassment that washed through her. She came so close to snatching the panties from his hand, but she wasn't about to give him the satisfaction of knowing that he was right about her. That she was different now. Stiff and uptight and *good*.

"I like tan."

"Seems to me like you've got a hankering for black." He eyed the panties. "Me, too." He stuffed them into his shirt pocket and glanced around. "Tan's a little boring. I'd go with something a little bolder. Maybe yellow. Brighten the place up."

"I don't need brighter. I need reliable." Her gaze narrowed. "Is that why you stopped by? To offer decorating advice?"

"Actually—" his voice took on a softer note "—I wanted to talk to you about last night."

"There's nothing to talk about. It's over and done with."

"That's the point." His mouth crooked in the faintest grin. "It's not."

"What makes you say that?"

"Because I want you and you still want me."

"Speak for yourself."

His gaze caught and held hers. "So you haven't been thinking about me kissing you or you touching me or me sliding deep, *deep* inside?" His eyes darkened as he reached out to finger the collar of her charcoal blouse. "One night isn't enough." His fingertip dipped beneath the neck and traced her collar bone. "We need to do it again. And again. However many times it takes."

"For what?"

"For me to stop thinking about me kissing you and you touching me and me sliding deep, *deep* inside. For you to forget, too."

"What makes you think I haven't already?"

"Because your cheeks are flushed and your pulse is erratic." He pressed a fingertip to the side of her neck in a slow sweeping gesture that sent goose bumps chasing up and down her arms. "And you look a little faint."

She felt a little faint. And flushed. And completely erratic.

"You're turned on."

He was right. Despite the fact that she'd cut loose last night, she was no closer to being free of the fantasies that haunted her night after night. If anything, she was even more worked up. Desperate. Hungry.

Still…she couldn't just hop back into bed with Jesse. She was the mayor, for heaven's sake. She had a town to run. Commitments. Car washes and bake sales and quilting circles.

Okay, so she wasn't actually running anything at the moment. Not until the day of the inauguration. Then her life would officially become a series of city council meetings, park dedications and press conferences. Ugh.

She swallowed the sudden bitterness in her mouth and focused on the man standing in front of her. For now, the only thing she *had* to do was put in a few personal appearances, which meant she had a few precious days to forget about what she needed to do and simply do what she *wanted* to do—play out the bad-girl fantasies that had been driving her crazy for the past twelve years and store enough memories to last her the rest of her boring, predictable life as mayor.

"Okay." The word was out before she could stop it. Not that she would have. She was doing this. She *wanted* to do this. Her gaze met his and a ripple of excitement went through her. "Let's do it again."

A grin played at his lips. "And again." His expression faded and there was nothing teasing about his next words. "I've got until Sunday. Pete gets hitched Saturday night and I head for Austin on Sunday morning."

And she would take her oath of office a full week after that.

She licked her lips and trembled at the anticipation

that rippled through her. "So, um, when should we start? I could meet you tonight after the Little League game. I'm throwing out the opening pitch—"

"Let's go," he cut in.

"Now?"

"Unless you need to practice for that pitch?" He arched an eyebrow, a grin playing at his lips.

"It's just ceremony. Accuracy isn't a big factor."

He motioned to the window and the jacked-up black pickup that sat out front. "Then what do you say we take a little ride?"

Meaning dripped from his words and for a split second, she hesitated. There was just something about the way he looked at her—as if he'd been waiting for this moment even longer than she had—that sent a spiral of fear through her. Because the last thing she wanted was to unlock any of her old feelings for Jesse.

This wasn't about the past. It was about this moment. He wanted her and she wanted him and once they'd satisfied that want completely, it would all be over. It was Tuesday and he was leaving Sunday. That meant they had five days.

The realization stirred a wave of anxiety as she felt the precious seconds ticking away. "Let's go."

11

THEY ENDED UP on a dusty back road that wound its way up to a steep cliff overlooking the lake. Lucky's Point had once been the hottest make-out spot back in the day. The spot, in fact, where she'd made out with Jesse James Chisholm for the very first time. Times had changed and the kids now hung out down below on the banks of Lost Gun River, and so the Point was deserted when they rolled to a stop a few feet away from the edge.

Still...this wasn't what she'd signed up for.

"I thought we were going to the motel," she said as he swung the truck around and backed up to the edge of the cliff.

"And fight our way past the reporters camped out on my doorstep?" He spared her a glance before killing the engine. "I thought you wanted to keep this low-key."

"I do. That's why I thought we'd go someplace a little more private to do the deed."

"Sugar, there's not a soul up here." He climbed out and went to lower the tailgate.

"That's not altogether true," she said as she followed him around to the back of the truck.

The sharp drop-off overlooked a spectacular view of the canyon and the rippling water. A huge bonfire blazed on the riverbank below. Ice chests were scattered here and there and dozens of teenagers milled about. Trucks lined the edge of the dirt road leading up to the gathering. Jason Aldean blasted from one of the truck radios, his rich, deep voice telling the tale of a dirt road just like the one that wound its way to the river.

"They won't bother you if you don't bother them." He winked and patted the spot on the tailgate next to him. "Climb up."

She hesitated, but then he touched her hand and she couldn't help herself. She climbed up and settled next to him.

He shifted his attention to the scene spread out before them. "It's still just as pretty as ever up here."

Her gaze followed the direction of his and she drank in the scene. A strange sense of longing went through her. It really was beautiful. Picturesque.

She dodged the thought and focused on the frantic beat of her own heart and the six feet plus of warm, hard male camped out next to her. "I'm surprised you remember." She slid him a sideways glance. "If memory serves, you didn't spend much time enjoying the view."

A grin tugged at his lips. "Oh, I enjoyed it plenty. It just didn't have much to do with the canyon."

"You were pretty fixated on one thing back then."

"Yeah." His gaze caught and held hers. "You." The word hung between them for a long moment and she had the crazy thought that he wasn't just talking about the past.

That he still felt something for her despite the fact that she'd walked away from him and ruined all their plans.

Crazy.

This was about lust and nothing else. Sex.

Thankfully.

"Thirsty?" His deep voice distracted her from the dangerous path her thoughts were taking.

She nodded. The truck rocked as he slid off the tailgate to retrieve a cooler from the cab.

She drew several deep breaths and damned herself for not insisting he take her to a motel. At the same time, she couldn't deny that he had a point. Last night had been fast and furious and much too fleeting. Maybe they did need to take their time and ease into things. Enjoy the moment.

The notion sent a burst of excitement through her almost as fierce as what she felt when he actually touched her. Her body tingled and her nipples pebbled and heat rippled along her nerve endings.

"It's awful hot." His deep voice drew her attention as he walked back, beers in hand.

And how.

She took the bottle he offered her and held tight to the ice-cold brew. The glass was hard and cold beneath her fingertips, a welcome relief against her blazing-hot skin.

He hefted himself back onto the tailgate. Metal shifted and rocked and his thigh brushed hers. A wave of heat sizzled through her. The urge to lean over and press her lips to his hit her hard and heavy and she leaned forward. Laughter drifted from below and her blood rushed that much faster before she caught herself.

She couldn't do this in front of an audience. She wouldn't. Even if the notion didn't bother her half as much as it should have.

Because it didn't bother her.

The old Gracie would have jumped at it.

She shifted her attention away from Jesse and focused straight ahead. The sun was just setting and the sky was a spray of oranges and reds. "The view really is something. I can see why they call it Lucky's Point. I'm sure many a girl gave it up just because of the ambiance."

"Actually, this spot was named for Lucky Wellsbee. He was an outlaw back in the late 1800s. He was on the run from Texas marshals after a stagecoach robbery when they cornered him right here. Legend says he took a nosedive off the edge of this cliff and was never seen or heard from again."

"Did he drown in the river?"

"Probably. Still, they never recovered a body and so no one really knows." He shrugged and twisted the cap off his own beer. "Anyhow, that's where the name really came from." He took a swig. "Though your version is a damned sight more fun." He grinned and the expression was infectious.

She felt a smile tug at her own lips. She took a pull on her beer and stared at the scene before her, her mind completely aware of the man sitting only inches away. As anxious as she was to get down to business, there was something oddly comforting about the silence that stretched between them, around them, twining tighter, pulling them closer. As if they were old friends who'd shared this exact moment time and time again.

They had.

The thought struck and she pushed it back out. Jesse wasn't her friend. Not now. Not ever again.

Even so, a strange sense of camaraderie settled between them as they sat there for the next few moments. She sipped her beer while he downed the rest of his. One last swig and he sat the bottle between them. It toppled onto its side with a clink, and suddenly a memory made her smile.

"Remember that time we played Truth or Dare?" The question was out before she could remind herself that the past was better left alone. "It was back before we started dating. Back when we were sophomores and you barely noticed me."

"Honey, any man with eyes noticed you. You didn't exactly go out of your way *not* to get noticed."

"I *did* wear my shirts a little too tight, didn't I? And my shorts a little too short." A smile tugged at her lips. "It used to drive my aunt and uncle nuts."

"Which is exactly why you did it."

"A fat lot of good it did." She shrugged. "I did my damnedest to fight destiny, but I guess in the end, she won anyway."

"Or you let her."

"What's that supposed to mean?"

"That sometimes it's a lot less work living up to people's expectations than it is changing their minds." He gave her a pointed look. "Nothing's written in stone. Take me for instance. I could have followed in my old man's footsteps, but I didn't. I made my own destiny. You gave in to yours."

"I didn't have a choice." The words were out before she could stop them. "When my brother passed away…" Her throat tightened. "I couldn't just run off and leave my sister when she needed me most." She blinked back the sudden stinging behind her eyes. "I couldn't."

She could still remember the funeral and her brother's closed casket. Charlie had held tight, clinging to Gracie, desperate for some stability.

And that was what Gracie had given her.

"I should have told you that instead of just cutting things off between us." She wasn't sure why she said the words, except that they'd been burning inside of her for so long that she couldn't help herself. "I'm sorry about that." The memories of those first few weeks after the funeral raced through her and her heart ached at the loss. Of her brother. Her freedom. Jesse. "You deserved an explanation when I bailed on you, not the cold shoulder." She stopped there because she couldn't tell him she'd been afraid to face him, to talk to him, so fearful she would change her mind the moment she saw him because she'd been hopelessly, madly in love with him.

Then.

Because they'd had so much in common. They'd shared the same hopes and dreams. The same desperation to escape the labels of a small town.

But now? She was different, even if she did feel the same flutter in the pit of her stomach when his deep voice slid into her ears.

"It was at one of Marilyn Marshall's parties, right? That time we played Truth or Dare?"

She nodded. "The one right after the homecoming

dance." A smile played at her lips as she remembered the short red Lycra dress she'd worn that night. She'd been crazy for that dress even though her aunt and uncle had hated it, just as she'd been crazy for a certain tall, sexy boy in faded jeans, scuffed boots and a T-shirt that said Save a Horse, Ride a Cowboy. "I can still remember her making us all sit in a circle. Kevin Baxter kept landing on me and daring me to play Seven Minutes in Heaven in Marilyn's closet."

"But you didn't."

"I didn't want to go into that closet with him. I wanted to go inside with you." She shrugged. "But when it was my turn, it kept landing on the wrong person."

He eyed the bottle and his eyes gleamed with challenge. "Maybe you'll have better luck now."

Reason told her to turn him down. Cutting loose behind closed doors was one thing, but this… This was different. This was talking and reminiscing and… *No.*

She didn't need a walk down memory lane with Jesse Chisholm.

But, oh, how she wanted one.

She met his gaze and reached for the bottle. A loud *thunk, thunk, thunk* echoed as she sent the glass spinning across the tailgate. Slowly it came to a stop, the mouth pointing directly at Jesse.

"Truth or dare?" she asked him.

His eyes twinkled. "Dare."

"I dare you to kiss me."

"Whatever happened to Seven Minutes in Heaven?"

"There's no closet, so I thought I'd adjust accordingly."

"We don't need a closet for heaven, sugar. We can

do it right here." No sooner had the words slipped past his lips than the truck dipped and he pushed to his feet. "Right now."

Before she could take her next breath, he stood directly in front of her, pure sin twinkling in his violet eyes.

He nudged her knees apart and stepped between her legs. Anticipation rippled through her as he leaned close. His warm breath tickled her bottom lip and her mouth opened.

"Relax," he murmured a split second before he touched her shoulders and urged her back down. The cold metal of the truck bed met her back and reality zapped her. There was no stifling darkness to hide her excitement. No closet walls to shield her from the rest of the world.

They were outside, in full view of God and at least a dozen teenagers partying on the riverbank below.

He reached for the waistband of her skirt. He tugged her zipper down, his gaze locked with hers.

"I think a kiss would be better," Gracie blurted, her anxiety getting the best of her. Jason Aldean had faded and Luke Bryan took his place, crooning about love and lust and leaving, and her heart beat that much faster.

"Oh, I'm going to kiss you, all right." He unfastened the skirt and pushed the material up around her waist, his fingers grazing the supersensitive skin of her stomach. "Just not on the lips. Not yet."

The sultry promise chased the oxygen from her lungs as he urged her legs apart and wedged himself between her knees. His fingertips swept her calves, up the outside of her knees until his hands came to rest on her thighs.

He touched his mouth to the inside of her thigh just a few inches shy of her panties. White cotton this time with tiny pink flowers. Sensible, or so she'd thought when she'd tugged them on that morning. But damned if she didn't feel just as sexy as when she'd worn the black lace the night before.

He nibbled and licked and worked his way slowly toward the heart of her. She found herself opening her legs even wider, begging him closer.

He trailed his tongue over the thin fabric covering her wet heat and pushed the material into her slit until her flesh plumped on either side. He licked and nibbled at her until her entire body wound so tight she thought she would shatter at any moment.

She didn't.

She couldn't.

Not until she felt him, skin to skin, flush against her body. No barriers between them. That was what she really wanted despite their location.

Because of it.

Being outside filled her with a sense of freedom she hadn't felt in a long, long time.

She ignored the thought as soon as it struck and focused on the large hands gripping her panties.

She lifted her hips to accommodate him. The cotton eased down her legs and landed on the truck bed next to her.

He caught her thighs and pulled her toward the end of the tailgate until her bottom was just shy of the edge. Grabbing her ankles, he urged her knees over his shoulders.

He slid his large hands beneath her buttocks and tilted her just enough. Dipping his head, he flicked his tongue along the seam between her slick folds in a long slow lick that sucked the air from her lungs.

His tongue parted her and he lapped at her sensitive clit. He tasted and savored, his tongue stroking, plunging, driving her mindless until she came apart beneath him. A cry vibrated from her throat and mingled with the sounds drifting from below.

Her heart beat a frantic pace for the next few moments as she tried to come to terms with what had just happened.

She'd had the mother of all orgasms. An orgasm worthy of the most erotic dream.

But as satisfied as she felt, it still wasn't enough.

She opened her eyes to find him staring down at her. A fierce look gleamed in his bright violet eyes, one that said he wanted to toss her over his shoulder, tote her home and never, ever let her go.

A spurt of warmth went through her.

Followed by a rush of panic because it was all just the heat of the moment.

He *would* let her go, and then he would leave. That was why she'd agreed to this in the first place. A few days of lust and then they both walked away. She headed for City Hall and he headed for Austin.

My turn.

That was what she wanted to say, but she wouldn't. While she'd agreed to indulge her lust for him, she had no intention of unleashing the bad girl that she'd locked down deep all those years ago. Giving in to him was one thing, but turning the tables and taking charge?

Not happening.

"Stand up," he murmured, killing the push-pull of

emotion inside of her and taking the decision out of her hands, and she quickly obliged.

She slid to her feet to stand in front of him. Her skirt fell back down her thighs, covering the fact that her panties still hung on the edge of his tailgate.

A fact he was all too aware of, if the tense set to his jaw was any indication.

He stood in front of her, his eyes gleaming in the growing shadows that surrounded them. His muscles bunched beneath his T-shirt. Taut lines carved his face, making him seem harsh, fierce, *hungry.*

She knew the feeling.

She swallowed against the sudden hollowness in her throat and fought to keep from reaching for the top button on her blouse. But then he murmured "Undress," and she quickly obliged.

She slid the first button free, then the next and the next, until the silky material parted. A quick shrug and the blouse slid down her shoulders, her arms, to glide from her fingertips and pool at her feet.

Her fingers went to the clasp of her bra. A quick flick and the cups sagged. The lace fell away and his breath hitched. His gaze darkened and his nostrils flared as if he couldn't get enough oxygen.

Her lips parted as she tried to drag some much-needed air into her own lungs. Her breasts heaved and his eyes sparkled, reflecting the last few rays of sunlight.

She touched the waistband of her skirt. Trembling fingers worked at the catch until the edges finally parted. She pushed the fabric down her legs and suddenly she was completely naked. Warm summer air slithered over her skin, amping up the heat already swamping her from the inside out.

"Damn, but you're beautiful, Gracie." The words were reverent and her heart beat that much faster, drowning out the sounds coming from below until the only thing she focused on was him and the way he was looking at her and the way it made her feel.

Sexy.

Alive.

Free.

"You're not done." His deep voice sent excitement rippling down her spine.

"I don't have any clothes left."

"I do. Take them off."

She stepped forward to grasp the hem of his T-shirt. Flesh grazed flesh as she obliged him, pushing the material up his ripped abdomen, over his shoulders and head, until it fell away and joined her discarded clothes. A brief hesitation and she reached for the waistband of his jeans.

A groan rumbled from his throat as her fingertips trailed over the denim-covered bulge. She worked the zipper down, tugging and pulling until the teeth finally parted. The jeans sagged on his hips, and his erection sprang hot and pulsing into her hands.

She traced the ripe purple head before sliding her hand down his length, stroking, exploring. His dark flesh throbbed against her palm and her own body shuddered in response. She licked her lips and fought the urge to drop to her knees and taste him.

Luckily, he wasn't nearly as restrained.

He drew her to him and kissed her roughly, his tongue delving deep into her mouth over and over until

the ground seemed to tilt. And then he swept her up,
laid her on the tailgate of his truck and plunged deep,
deep inside.

12

SHE STILL HAD her panties.

Gracie held tight to the knowledge as she slipped inside her house later that night. The steady hum of a motor out front reminded her that Jesse still hadn't pulled away yet.

Which meant she could easily forget the fact that she had to crawl out of bed before the crack of dawn in order to make it to Wednesday Waffles, the Senior Ladies' weekly gathering. She was scheduled to recite the opening Pledge of Allegiance and serve the first waffle. Not a bad gig except half the group was diabetic and the other half had intestinal trouble. Forget stacks of fluffy golden squares topped with whipped cream and chocolate chips. The waffles were all-bran, served with sugar-free syrup and Myrtle Nell's infamous prune compote.

Which meant instead of counting down the hours until tomorrow morning, Gracie would much rather haul open the door, throw herself at the cowboy idling in her driveway and beg for round two.

And three.

An all-nighter, as a matter of fact.

The urge gripped her and her hands trembled, but then Sugar Lips scrambled from the kitchen. Her claws slid across the hardwood floor in a frantic scrape as she rushed for the door.

Bran was good. Healthy.

Gracie latched onto that all-important fact and scooped up the white ball of fluff. The dog licked at her frantically for a few seconds before her high-pitched barks filled the air. Gracie set her on the floor and she danced in place for a few seconds before leading the way to the kitchen and the treat jar.

Gathering her control, Gracie forced herself away from the front door and followed Sugar Lips into the kitchen. She unearthed Sugar's favorite powdered do-nuts from the cabinet and fed one to the frantic animal.

The dog wolfed down the goody and barked and danced for another.

"One a day. You know the rule."

Rules. That was what life was all about. About re-specting boundaries and walking the straight and nar-row and playing it safe. That was who she was now, even if Jesse had made her forget that all-important fact for those few blissful moments at the river.

She was still the Gracie who ate granola for break-fast every morning and wore conservative shoes and spent her Saturday nights in front of the TV. She wasn't wild and wicked.

Even if she had worn a black lace thong to the of-fice yesterday. Sexy lingerie was her one indulgence. Pretty undies and lacy bras. Even the white cotton bi-kini panties she'd worn tonight were on the risqué side.

Which explained her thoughts at the moment.

The underwear. She needed to tame it down in a major way, which meant that first thing tomorrow she was going to do some online shopping for some sensible lingerie. Some Spanx and granny panties and boxy bras.

You're still as out of control as ever.

He was wrong and he would see that soon enough.

She intended to make him see that, to keep the emotional wall as strong as ever between them so that when Sunday rolled around, it would be that much easier to say goodbye.

Because Gracie Stone didn't want a forever with Jesse Chisholm. She wanted to get him out of her head. Her fantasies.

Once and for all.

That meant keeping her guard up, holding back and showing him she'd turned into a bona fide good girl.

He would gladly call it quits then and run the other way once he realized she truly had changed.

She just wished that fact didn't suddenly bother her so much.

HE WANTED MORE.

The thought echoed in Jesse's head as he sat outside the modest brick home a few blocks over from City Hall, his engine idling, his blood racing.

While they'd just gotten down and dirty in the bed of his pickup, they hadn't come close to burning up the lust that blazed between them. He still felt every bit as restless. As hungry.

Not that he intended to do anything more about it tonight. He had to be up early tomorrow morning for a training session and he had no intention of letting their agreement get in the way of his next championship.

His heartbeat kicked up a notch as the lights flipped on inside and he watched her shadow move across the first-floor window. A vision played in his head and he saw her pushed up against a nearby wall, her legs wrapped around his waist. Her hands clawed at his shoulders and her tits bounced as he pumped into her and—

Awww, *hell.*

His gut tensed and his dick throbbed. He tightened one hand on the steering wheel and shoved the truck into Reverse with his other. With a squeal of tires, he pulled out of her driveway and headed for the motel.

Five minutes later, he sat idling in the parking lot, his attention fixed on the photographer camped out on the doorstep of his room. He'd expected the two from last night, but this guy was new. And probably just another in a long line he was sure to encounter over the next few days.

He thought of calling the front desk but then changed his mind. He could have this guy escorted off the property, but there would just be another to take his place. Better to give them what they wanted, answer a few questions and let them have their photo op, which was what he fully intended to do.

Just not tonight.

He turned his pickup around and headed for the training facility that sat outside of town. Ten minutes later he pulled into the gravel parking lot and killed the engine. He headed for the exterior staircase that led to a small apartment over the main office. During rodeo time, the competing cowboys used the spot to unwind or catch a nap in between rides. With a window that overlooked the main arena, they could enjoy the other events while kicking back and conserving their strength.

The place sat dark and quiet now.

Jesse flipped on a switch and the overhead light chased away the dark shadows, revealing a large living space complete with a living room, a fully equipped kitchen and a bathroom. Jesse was just about to head for the bathroom and a nice cold shower when he saw a flicker of light beyond the wall of windows overlooking the dark arena.

He closed the distance to the glass and sure enough, a light bobbed in the far distance near the animal pens.

A few minutes later he rounded the first bull pen to find Troy spread out on a blanket, an iPod in one hand and a magazine in the other. The minute he saw Jesse, he snatched the headphones out of his ears. The magazine slapped together as he scrambled to his feet.

"What are you doing?"

"W-working late," Troy blurted. "Eli wants us to clean out the pens first thing tomorrow. I thought I'd get a jump on it tonight."

"So you're here this late to clean pens?"

"Actually, I thought I'd just crash here and get an early start."

"And your folks are okay with you sleeping here?"

"My mom is dead. A car wreck about eight years ago." He shrugged. "My dad doesn't care what I do. The only thing he cares about is getting drunk. He's on a bender right now." His gaze met Jesse's. "If you let me stay here tonight, I promise I'll be up before anyone gets here. I'll even shovel all the stalls myself."

"A car wreck, huh?"

Troy nodded. "She was on her way home from work."

"My mom died when I was four," Jesse murmured. "She had complications when she had my youngest brother. My dad was never much of a dad, either."

"A drunk?"

"Among other things." He eyed the blanket. "But you can't sleep here."

Troy's head snapped up and his gaze collided with Jesse's. "Please, Mr. Chisholm. I won't get in the way. I promise."

Jesse shook his head. "As much as I'd like to let you sleep right here, I'm afraid I can't. If you start snoring, you might spook the bulls." The kid actually looked ready to cry until Jesse added, "I'm bunking out in the small apartment upstairs, but there's a pullout couch in the main office. Clean sheets in the cabinet. You can sleep there."

"Really?"

Jesse nodded. "But only if you promise to get up five minutes early and put on a pot of coffee. If you're camping out in the office, you're in charge of the coffee machine."

"I promise."

"Get some sleep, then." Jesse motioned toward the office. "I'll see you tomorrow."

Troy snatched up his blanket and magazine and made a beeline for the office. A smile played at his lips and Jesse's chest tightened.

He knew exactly what Troy was feeling at the moment. He'd felt it himself every night when his dad had been three sheets to the wind and he and his brothers had bedded down in the old Buick just to get away from the chaos.

Relief.

Bone-deep, soothing relief because he didn't have to worry about waking to a drunken rant or picking his dad up off the bathroom floor or winding up on the opposite end of his fist. For tonight, Troy was safe.

If only Jesse felt the same at the moment.

Instead, he was on edge. Wired. Desperate.

And all because of Gracie.

Yep, he wanted more, all right. And he had only four days to get it, because he was leaving first thing Sunday morning.

That meant he was going to have to spend a lot of time with her between now and then, more than just the proposed sneaking around after hours, that was for damned sure. No, Jesse needed to *overindulge* if he meant to get Gracie out of his system and lay the past to rest once and for all.

He had to.

Because Jesse was finally moving on with his life. But in order to move on, he needed to let go of the past.

Of Gracie.

He would.

But first he was going to haul her close and hold on tight.

13

When Gracie walked into City Hall on Wednesday morning, she was more than happy to find Trina ready and waiting with a full day's itinerary. After a sleepless night spent reliving her encounter with Jesse, she needed something—anything—to get her mind off what had happened and how much she'd liked it.

And how she couldn't wait until it happened again.

But she would wait because she had responsibilities. Places to go. People to see. Waffles to eat.

High-fiber bran waffles that looked like cardboard and tasted even more bland.

"These are interesting," she said to the blue-haired woman sitting across from her.

"Don't be silly, child. They taste terrible like that." Myrtle Nell, president of the Senior Ladies' Auxiliary and chairperson for the brunch, handed Gracie a bowl filled with a dark brown jellylike substance. "You need the prune compote on top to really bring out the flavor."

"Wow. This looks yummy." *Not.* Gracie watched as

the woman heaped a few spoonfuls onto her plate and tried not to make a face.

"It's homemade." Myrtle motioned her to take another bite and Gracie had the sudden urge to run. Away from the waffles and the gossip.

Straight to Jesse.

She ditched the thought, forced herself to take a bite and tuned in to the conversation flying back and forth across the table.

She learned all about Carl Simon's new hair plugs and Janet Green's collagen injections and Helen Culpepper's latest affair with some rancher from nearby Rusk County.

Carl had developed a massive infection from the plugs that no amount of antibiotic cream could touch. Janet had overdone the treatment and now looked like a blowfish. And Helen's latest fling was a huge *Brokeback Mountain* fan.

The only thing she didn't hear about was any mention of her run-in with Jesse in front of the bakery. Not that the entire town wasn't privy to the information. They were, but they'd obviously written it off as a friendly exchange between politician and constituent.

That should have been enough to ease Gracie's nerves. She was still worked up after a sleepless night spent replaying her evening with Jesse. Want gripped her, but she tamped it back down. She had obligations first. Responsibilities.

Which was why she forced down not one but two waffles before she headed over to the seventh-grade car wash.

"I'm ready to work," she told Shirley Buckner, the fortysomething English teacher and supervisor for the fundraising event. Shirley wore blue-jean capris, a Lost Gun Middle School T-shirt and a haggard expression that said she needed a giant margarita a lot more than a helping hand.

She handed Gracie a bucket and directed her over to a dust-covered Chevy four-door pickup truck with the familiar Cartwright Ranch logo on the side. "You can start on Lloyd Cartwright's truck. He brought in all six of them." She indicated the row of matching vehicles that spanned the length of the middle school parking lot.

"Oh, and smile." Shirley lifted the camera that hung around her neck as an afterthought and clicked a picture. "Great. Now get moving."

"Shouldn't you take off the lens cap first?" Gracie pointed to the covering on the high-dollar camera similar to the one she'd had back in the day.

"A cap?" Shirley eyed the contraption as if seeing it for the first time. Her eyebrows drew together into a frown as she twisted the covering. The cap popped off into her hands. "Great. Just friggin' great. I've shot over forty pictures in the past hour. All for nothing." She grabbed the walkie-talkie from her belt. "Charlene? Is June still in the bathroom?"

"I sent her home. She's *really* sick."

"Great. Just friggin' *great*."

"June?" Gracie eyed the teacher. "June Silsbee? The reporter from the newspaper?"

Shirley nodded. "She was here covering the event for the paper, but then she upchucked in the parking lot on account of she's pregnant with triplets. She and Martin did that in vitro thing. Anyhow, she handed me her camera and made a beeline for the restroom.

I haven't seen her since." She eyed the camera. "The kids are so excited. The paper promised us front-page coverage, which we're counting on because the car wash itself never brings in quite enough money. But then the paper comes out and we get a rush of donations from local businesses." She shook her head. "But none of that's going to happen, since I can't even work this blasted thing."

"I can." The words were out before Gracie could stop them. Not that she would have. Her gaze shifted to the dozens of kids piled around a nearby car. They worked diligently, scrubbing and laughing. She ignored the doubt that rippled deep inside and gave in to the grin tugging at her lips. "Hand it over and I'll see what I can do."

She spent the next hour taking picture after picture while the kids sprayed and washed and got each other wet. She was just about to snap a pic of the girls choir group serenading one of the customers when she caught sight of a familiar pair of Wranglers in her peripheral vision.

She turned in time to see Jesse slam the door shut on his jacked-up pickup truck. He wore a fitted white T-shirt and faded jeans that hugged his muscles to perfection and tugged at the seams as he started toward her.

What the hell?

He wasn't supposed to be here. Not now. They'd made arrangements to meet tonight at his motel room. He wasn't supposed to be here in full view of everyone. Especially not looking so downright sexy. Her stomach hollowed out and she had the sudden urge to throw herself into his arms and kiss him for all she was worth. In front of God and the entire Lost Gun seventh grade.

"Excuse me." She snatched the water hose out of a nearby girl's hand and before she could think better of it, she let loose a stream of water directly in Jesse's direction. He sputtered and frowned, and she put her back to him, giving herself a silent high five for marksmanship.

Now he would turn and head the other way.

That was what she told herself, but then she heard his deep voice directly behind her.

"What the hell are you doing?"

She whirled and tried to look surprised. "Oh, my. Did I get you wet? You must have walked into my line of fire."

"I didn't do any such thing. I was your line of fire."

"Don't be silly." She tried to laugh off the coincidence, but he wasn't buying it. She finally shrugged. "So I got you a little wet. Stop making such a big fuss."

"A little wet?" He arched an eyebrow at her, amusement dancing in his violet eyes before they darkened and the air stalled in her lungs. "I'm soaked to the bone, in case you haven't noticed."

She'd noticed, all right. His white T-shirt, now practically transparent, stuck to him like a second skin, showing off every bulge and ripple of his broad shoulders and sinewy chest. She could even see the shadow of hair that circled his nipples and funneled down his abdomen. "At least I'm in good company." He nodded at her.

She became acutely aware of the glide of water down her own neck, the sticky wetness of her silk blouse plastered against her chest. A glance down and she realized her aim hadn't been that great. Her own clothing was in no better shape than his, her shirt practically transparent, revealing the lacy bra she wore and the puckered tips of her breasts. Her only consolation? The high-dollar camera hanging around her neck, the strap plunging between her perky nipples, was waterproof.

"It's a car wash." She bristled. "People get wet. It's a hazard of the job." She grasped for a change of subject. "What are you doing here?"

"I thought I'd pick you up and we could have lunch."

"Here? In town?"

"Why not?"

"Because you hate this town."

He shrugged. "A man's gotta eat. So what do you say?"

"I'd say your timing sucks. As you can see, I'm busy."

"Oh, I see, all right." He eyed her wet blouse and his smile widened. "You look good wet." His deep voice stirred something even worse than the sudden panic beating at her senses. "But then I already knew that." Excitement flowered inside her, making her heart pound and her blood rush.

She felt herself melting beneath the warmth in his eyes, his smile, and so she did what any freedom-loving woman would have done. She squirted him again for good measure, ignored the urge to snatch a picture of him soaked to his skin, turned on her heel and walked away.

Walked being the key word when all she really wanted to do was run. Because as much as Jesse excited her, he scared the crap out of her, too. The way he smiled. The way he made her feel when he smiled.

This feeling was not part of her plan. Working him

out of her system to gain some much-needed closure—definitely tops on her agenda. But this warm, achy feeling? The urge to shirk her duties, climb into the cab of his pickup truck and drive off into the sunset?

No.

No matter how hot the temperature, how hot his gaze or how hot the heat that burned between them. This was strictly sex.

Closure sex.

Unfortunately, she wasn't used to any kind of sex, which explained why she couldn't forget Jesse James Chisholm or his damnable grin the rest of the afternoon after she dropped off the camera to the newspaper office and headed back to City Hall.

She turned her attention to unpacking the boxes of books back at her office and sliding them onto the newly delivered shelves. Unfortunately, it wasn't enough to make her forget Jesse or the upcoming evening.

He was there in her head, teasing and tempting and reminding her of last night. Of how much she still wanted him.

She found herself counting down the seconds until she could see him again.

Because he'd awakened her long-deprived hormones and so, of course, he was starring in a few crazy fantasies. But that was all they were. No way did Gracie actually want to ride off into the sunset with Jesse. She wasn't riding anywhere. She was here in Lost Gun to stay.

And Jesse wasn't.

Sunday.

The word echoed in her head, fueling her resolve

as she picked up the phone and dialed his number. His voice mail picked up.

"I'm afraid I've got a late meeting. I'll have to take a rain check tonight. Talk to you tomorrow."

There. No matter how much she might want him, she didn't need him.

That was what she told herself as she slid the books into place, one after the other, until the shelf was full.

Like her life. Full. Content. She didn't want for anything.

OKAY, SO MAYBE she wanted for one thing. A way past Big Earl's trio of pit bulls.

"I need the biggest steak you've got," she told the butcher the next morning after a night of tossing and turning and surfing late-night cable TV.

She'd ended up on Animal Planet watching a *K9 Cops* marathon. After twelve back-to-back episodes and four packs of Life Savers, she'd hit on an idea.

"Rib eye? New York strip? Filet?" asked Merle Higgam, the head butcher at the local Piggly Wiggly.

"Yes."

"Yes to which one?"

"All three." She wasn't sure which cut would go over best with the vicious trio, so she didn't want to take any chances. "Just make sure they're all really thick."

Ten minutes later she climbed into her car with the freezer-wrapped package and headed over to Big Earl's. Trina had reported back that Big Earl was even older and more decrepit than they remembered. No way could he actually be making moonshine again.

At the same time, Gracie needed to see for herself. To warn him what would happen if he violated his probation.

"Lookie here, big boy," Gracie said, summoning her sultriest "come and get me" voice as she held one of her purchases over the fence and did her best to entice the first animal that poked his head out of an oversize doghouse. "I've got something *really* special for you."

He barked once, twice, before making a mad dash for her. She tossed the steak to her far left and waited while the other two dogs joined the first. Summoning her courage, she climbed over the fence and made a beeline for the house. She hit the front steps two at a time and did a fast knock on the door.

"Big Earl? It's me. Mayor Stone. I need to talk to you."

"Who is it?"

"Mayor Stone."

"Mayor who?"

"Stone."

"Sorry, I ain't got no phone."

"I didn't say phone. I said Stone."

"The mayor?"

"That's me."

"Ain't got no key, either. 'Sides, you don't need a key. The door's unlocked."

Gracie's fingers closed over the doorknob just as she heard the barking behind her. She chanced a glance over her shoulder to see one of the dogs catch sight of her. She pushed open the door and slammed it shut behind her just as Ferocious Number One raced for the porch, his jaws wagging, his teeth flashing.

Heart pounding, she turned to drink in the interior of the double-wide trailer. Wood paneling covered the walls. An old movie poster from *The Outlaw Josey Wales* hung over an old lumpy beige couch piled high with old lumpy pillows. A scarred mahogany coffee table sat stacked with crossword puzzles. In the far corner sat an old lumpy recliner with an old lumpy man parked on top.

The last time she had seen Big Earl had been at a Fourth of July picnic six years ago. He'd been in attendance with his great-granddaughter, Casey, who'd been helping Frank Higgins, the owner of the local gas station, set off the fireworks. Casey had just graduated high school. She'd been working for Frank at the time, pumping gas and cleaning windshields, and so he'd brought her along to help tote the fourteen boxes of sparklers and Roman candles he'd donated. That had been the night that Judge Ellis had bought a case of moonshine off of Big Earl and stashed it in the trunk of his Lexus, which had turned out to be the finale of the fireworks show.

Big Earl had been wearing the same red-and-white-checked shirt he had on now. Except the colors had been a lot more vibrant and the fabric a lot less wrinkled.

The old man had a head full of snow-white hair that was slicked back with pomade. His eyes were pale blue and enormous behind a pair of thick round glasses.

"Well, I'll be." Big Earl peered at her. "Don't just stand there, come on in." He waved a hand for her to sit down next to him, only the nearest chair was a good five feet away.

She eased onto the edge of the sofa across from him. "So?" Her gaze skittered around the room, from an old cuckoo clock that ticked away in the kitchen to the ancient movie poster. "How have you been?"

"Fair to midland, I s'pose. Why, back in the day I was as spry as a young spring chicken. I was into everything back then. Knew everybody's business. Had plenty of business of my own, if you know what I mean."

"About that…" she started, but Big Earl wasn't quite finished yet.

"But time sure has a way of slowin' a man down. Why, my back's been achin' somethin' fierce and I got these bunions. I've been doin' Epsom salts in my bath and that helps some."

"That's good to hear. Speaking of hearing, I was just wondering…" Her words faded off as she noticed the way his eyes fixed on the spot just over her left shoulder. As if he couldn't quite focus on her. She noticed the magnifying glass on the tray table next to him. And the extra batteries for his hearing aid. And a tube of arthritis cream.

She realized then that the only thing Big Earl could possibly cook up in his condition was a piece of burnt toast. The man could hardly see. Or hear. Or walk, judging by the cane propped next to him and the nearby walker parked in the corner. He certainly wasn't in any condition to measure out ingredients or tiptoe around and keep one eye out for the cops while maintaining watch over a highly combustible still.

He wagged a bent finger in her general vicinity. "So what is it you needed to talk to me about?"

Gracie shrugged. "Just checking in to see how you're doing."

He grinned a toothless grin. "Mighty nice of you.

Why, I ain't had visitors in years. Used to head into town once a week for bingo, but I cain't even do that anymore. Thank the good Lord for cable—otherwise I'd be bored out of my mind."

"You watch a lot of TV?"

"I mainly listen to it. Turn the volume up real loud on account of my hearin' ain't what it used to be. But I get by. Still catch my favorite shows. Never miss an episode of *The Rifleman* or *Bonanza.* I love those old Westerns."

Her gaze shifted to the movie poster. "You a Clint Eastwood fan?"

"I'm a Josey Wales fan. Eastwood ain't never done anything since that's worth a hill of beans."

"Now, remember, when things look bad and it looks like you're not gonna make it, then you gotta get mean." Gracie read the movie quote at the bottom of the poster. "Plumb mad-dog mean." There was something oddly familiar about the saying, but she couldn't quite place it.

"Words to live by." Big Earl grinned. "'Course, I ain't in much condition to get mean anymore, either. I leave that to my Casey. Girl's got a fiery streak that would make her mama proud. Why, she don't let no-body push her around. She ought to be back in a few minutes. Ran into town to pick up my foot cream."

"I'm sorry I missed her." Gracie pushed to her feet. "Maybe we can catch up next time."

"You sure you don't want to wait and say hello?"

"I really should get going." Her hand closed on the doorknob and she heard the growls coming from the other side. "On second thought—" she summoned a smile and sank back down onto the sofa "—I wouldn't want to be rude."

14

WHAT THE HELL was he doing here?

Gracie's hand faltered on the brownie she was stuffing into a plastic baggie. She stood behind one of the handful of tables set up on the lawn in front of City Hall. She set the treat aside, next to the dozen or so she'd just bagged for the annual Daughters of the Republic of Texas bake sale and did her best to calm her pounding heart.

Pounding, of all things. When she'd promised herself just last night after she'd cancelled on him that she wasn't going to get nervous. Or excited. Or turned on when she finally saw him again.

Especially turned on. She had a reputation to protect and salivating at the first sign of the town's hottest bad boy, particularly in front of the biggest busybodies in said town, was not in keeping with the conservative image of Lost Gun's newly elected mayor.

Tongues were already wagging about the car wash incident. Of course, they were all focused on the fact that Jesse James Chisholm had been wet and practically half-naked in front of every female teacher at the middle school rather than Gracie, who'd been the cause of it.

It was all Jesse's fault. He was too bold and much too sexy for his own good.

She forced an indifferent expression and tried to ignore the way his tight jeans hugged his muscular thighs as he approached her table. He wore a black T-shirt and a dusty cowboy hat that said he'd been in the middle of a training session not too long ago.

Yet here he was in the heart of Lost Gun.

"Brownie, cupcake or cheesecake bar?" she croaked when he reached her table.

"I'll take all three."

"Wow. Somebody's hungry."

"You have no idea."

She knew by the way his eyes darkened that he wasn't talking about the scrumptious goodies spread out on the table between them. She tamped down on her own growling stomach and reached for a white bakery bag. With trembling hands, she loaded his goodies inside and handed them over. "That'll be three dollars."

He pulled out his wallet and unfolded a ten. "Keep the change." Their hands brushed as she took the money and a jolt of electricity shot through her.

"Why did you cancel last night?"

"I was busy."

"Busy or scared?"

"Scared of what? Of you?" She shook her head. "I'm not scared of you."

"No." He eyed her for a silent moment. "You're scared of us," he finally said.

"There is no us. This isn't a long-term arrangement. You're leaving on Sunday." She didn't mean to sound so accusing. "Which is a good thing," she blurted. "A really good thing. Enjoy." She pushed the goodies in his direction and turned her attention to the next customer in line.

She glimpsed his handsome face in her peripheral vision, his eyes trained on her, his lips set in a grim line. As if he was thinking real hard about some question and he wasn't too pleased with the answer.

As if he wasn't any more happy to be here than she was to see him here.

She pondered the notion for a few seconds as she served up several more baggies of goodies and tried to pretend for all she was worth that his presence didn't affect her.

Fat chance.

Every nerve in her body was keenly aware of him. She felt his warm gaze on her profile and a slow heat swept over her, from the tips of her toes clear to the top of her head, until she all but burned in the midday heat. She shifted her stance, her thighs pressing together, and an ache shot through her. Her nipples pebbled, rubbing against her bra, and her fingers faltered on the pie she was about to slice.

The pie splattered to the ground at her feet and her heart slammed against her rib cage. She shoveled the gooey mess back into the pie plate and headed for the building and the small kitchen situated at the rear of City Hall, next to a large conference room being used for the monthly Daughters of the Texas Republic meeting immediately following the bake sale.

Inside the kitchen, the ladies had stored all of their extra sweets. There were rows of pies and cakes and cookies.

She dumped the peach mess into a nearby trash can and went to the sink to wash her hands. Her fingers trembled and the soap slipped from her grasp. "Damn it," she muttered.

"Careful, sugar. You'll have the ladies dropping to their knees for an impromptu prayer meeting."

The deep voice froze her hands.

Worse, Jesse leaned in, his arms coming around her on either side, his hands closing over hers to steady her as she reached for the bar of soap.

His large tanned hands were a stark contrast against her white fingers. His warm palms cradled the tops of her hands. The rough pads of his fingertips rasped against her soft flesh and heat spiraled through her body. His nearness was like a fuzzy blanket smothering the cold panic that had rolled through her the moment she'd realized that he'd followed her inside.

"Easy, now." His voice rumbled over her bare shoulder and warm breath brushed her skin. Goose bumps chased up and down her arms and she came close to leaning back into him, closing her eyes and enjoying the delicious sensation. Just for a little while.

She stiffened and fought for her precious control. Twelve years of cloaking herself in it should have made it easy to find, but not with Jesse so close. Too close for her to breathe, much less think, much less pretend.

"You have to cradle the bar of soap and slide it through your fingers like this." He slid his fingers over the slick bar and suds lathered between their fingers. "You have to go easy and slow." As he said the words, she got the distinct impression that he was talking about more than just washing her hands.

"Thanks for the advice, but no thanks. I do not need

to go slow and easy." To prove her point, she focused every ounce of energy she had on ignoring the delicious feelings assaulting her body. She held her breath and rolled the bar between her palms before shoving her hands under the spraying faucet.

His arms fell away as she turned off the water and reached for a dish towel. She scooted past him and headed for the large storage room that sat just behind the kitchen, eager to put as much distance as possible between them.

"What are you doing here?" she demanded when he followed her into the back room. She forced her face into the tightest frown she could manage, considering she wanted to kiss him more than she wanted her next breath.

"We made a deal. Sex," he murmured, the word rumbling up her spine.

"Not now. Not here." While she wanted Jesse, she wasn't supposed to want him. That meant no blushing or trembling or kissing. "There are too many people here."

"Why, there isn't a soul in sight." He glanced around to prove his point. A bare bulb hung overhead, illuminating the small room that housed everything from gallon cans of chili and beans to five-gallon jars of tomato sauce for the Senior Ladies weekly spaghetti night. The place stocked all of the supplies for any of the functions held in the main conference room next to the kitchen. Boxes of paper goods, from plates to napkin packets to disposable cups, lined a metal shelf that ran the length of one wall.

"This isn't a good idea." She turned her back on him, determined to forget his presence and keep her mind on the task at hand. She made her way to a six-foot table that held the rest of the goodies that the Ladies' Auxiliary had donated for today's luncheon. There were dozens of pies and platters of brownies and a few cakes. She was busy reading the masking tape labels on the tops of the plastic-wrapped goodies when she heard Jesse step up behind her again.

"This really isn't a good idea." She snatched up a carrot cake and turned, the confection smack-dab between them.

"Actually, I think it's a pretty fine idea." Jesse's deep voice sent a jolt of adrenaline through her. His eyes glittered with a hungry light that sucked the oxygen from her lungs and made her hands tremble. He caught the edge of the door that adjoined the kitchen and shut it behind him, closing them off from the rest of the world.

The cake slid from her grasp, landing in a pile of smashed frosting and plastic wrap at her feet. Ugh. That made not one but two desserts she'd killed on account of Jesse James Chisholm.

"You'd better get your checkbook ready to make a nice big fat donation." She knelt to retrieve the mess, but he was right beside her, his hands bumping hers as they both reached for the cardboard base at the same time.

"I'm not the one that keeps dropping everything."

"Because of you."

"Because you like what I do to you. You just don't want to admit it."

His hand stalled on hers and heat whispered up her arm. "I can't do this here."

"You don't have to *do* a thing." He reached for her

hands, which were now covered with frosting. Before she could draw her next breath, his tongue flicked out and he licked one finger. Once, twice, before sliding it deep in his mouth and suckling for a breath-stealing moment. "Just feel."

"I…" She swallowed and tried to think of something to say, but with his lips so firm and purposeful around her finger, his tongue rasping her skin, she couldn't seem to find any words. "Somebody might come looking for me," she managed to say several moments later after he'd licked her finger clean.

"You'll be back with more desserts in no time." He licked his lips, and she had the sudden image of him licking other parts of her body. Lapping at her neck and her nipples and her belly button and the wet heat between her legs. "But first I want my dessert."

Chatter drifted through the open doorway. The PA system crackled as it switched on and Myrtle's voice came over the loudspeaker as she tested the mic for the upcoming meeting. Even closer, the hum of the coffee machine drifted from inside the kitchen, along with the rush of water as someone flipped on a faucet. There were people just beyond the thin walls of the storage room. People starting to prep for the upcoming meeting. People who could walk in at any moment and find their mayor having dessert with the town's baddest bad boy.

She stiffened and forced aside the stirring images. "I really think we should wait until this evening. I'll meet you at the motel."

"You cancelled on me once. I won't take that chance again. Besides, I don't like to wait." He kissed her then, his lips wet and hungry, his tongue greedy as he devoured her.

"I don't think—" But then he fingered her nipple through the soft cotton of her shirt and she stopped thinking altogether.

He dropped to his knees in front of her, his hands going to her hips. He paused to knead her bottom through the fitted material of her skirt. Fabric brushed her legs as he slid it down over her thighs, her knees, until the skirt pooled on the floor.

He stood, then slid his hands around to her bottom and lifted her onto the counter. He paused only to grab one of the large wire racks filled with boxes and shove it in front of the door. It wasn't enough to keep anyone out should they really want to get in, but it was enough to buy them some time to grab their clothes should they be discovered.

Walking back to her, he wedged himself between her parted thighs. He urged her backward until her back met the countertop and then he slowly unbuttoned her shirt and unhooked the front clasp of her bra.

He fingered a dollop of frosting from the cake plate. "I really do like cream cheese," he murmured before touching the filling to one ripe nipple. He circled the tip, spreading the glaze until it covered her entire areola.

His gaze drilled into hers for a heart-stopping moment before he lowered his dark head. His tongue lapped at the side of her breast.

The licking grew stronger, more purposeful, as he gobbled up the white confection, starting at the outside and working his way toward the center. Sensation rippled up her spine.

The first leisurely rasp of his tongue against her ripe nipple wrung a cry from her throat. Her fingers threaded through his hair as he drew the quivering tip deep into his hot, hungry mouth. He suckled her long and hard and she barely caught the moan that tried to escape her throat.

She bit her lip as he licked and suckled and nipped. Her skin grew itchy and tight. Pressure started between her legs, heightened by the way he leaned into her, the hard ridge of his erection prominent beneath his jeans. She spread her legs wider and he settled more deeply between them. Grasping her hips, he rocked her.

Rubbed her.

Up and down and side to side and—

The shrill whistle of a tea kettle filled the air, penetrating the haze of pleasure that gripped her senses. Panic bolted through her and she went still.

"Wait." She grasped his muscled biceps to still his movements. "I need to go check the tea. If I don't, someone else will."

He leaned back, his gaze so deep and searching, as if he were doing his damnedest to see inside of her. "No," he finally murmured, his fingertip tracing the edge of her panties where elastic met the tender inside of her thigh. "You're not going anywhere. This isn't about going, sugar." His finger dipped into the steamy heat beneath. "It's about coming."

One touch of his callused fingertip against her swollen flesh and she arched up off the counter. She caught her bottom lip again and stifled a cry.

With a growl, he spread her wide with his thumb and forefinger and touched and rubbed as he dipped his head and drew on her nipple.

It was too much and not enough. She clamped her lips shut and forced her eyes open. But he was there, filling her line of vision, his fierce gaze drilling into hers. Searching and stirring and—

"Is somebody back there?" Lora Tremayne's voice echoed in the background, followed by the rattle of the doorknob as the president of the Daughters of the Republic of Texas tried to open the door to the storage room.

Gracie stiffened, her hands diving between them to stop the delicious stroke of his fingers.

As if he sensed her sudden resistance, his movements stilled. His chest heaved and his hair tickled her palms. Damp fingertips trailed over her cheek in a tender gesture that warmed her heart almost as much as her body.

"Come for me." His gaze was hot and bright and feverish as he stared down at her, into her. But there was something else, as well. A desperation that eased the panic beating at her senses and sent a rush of determination through her.

"Hello? Who's in there?"

It was Lora again, but it didn't matter. Gracie no longer cared if the entire Ladies' Auxiliary stood on the outside of the door, waiting and listening.

It wasn't about what everyone else thought about her. It was about him. What he thought about her. What he felt for her. What he wanted from her. What he *needed* from her.

And what she needed from him.

Her fingers dove into his front pocket and retrieved the small foil packet tucked there.

He answered her unspoken invitation by tugging

at the button on his jeans, pulling his zipper down and freeing his hard length. He opened the condom and spread it on his throbbing penis before leaning in closer, until the head pushed just a fraction of an inch inside of her.

Pleasure pierced her brain for a split second, quickly shattering into a swell of sensation as he filled her with one deep, probing thrust.

Her muscles convulsed around him, clutching him as he gripped her bare bottom. He pumped into her, the pressure and the friction so sweet that it took her breath away.

She was vaguely aware of the voices on the other side of the door. But then he touched her nipple and trailed a hand down her stomach, his fingertips making contact with the place where they joined, and all thought faded in a rush of sweet desire. She met his thrusts in a wild rhythm that urged him faster and deeper and…there. Right. *There!*

Her lips parted and she screamed at the blinding force of the climax that picked her up and turned her inside out. He caught the sound with his mouth and buried himself deep inside her one last time. A shudder went through him as he followed her over the edge.

She wrapped her arms around him and held him. Oddly enough, the fact that she would have to walk out of here with Jesse, past whoever had knocked on the door, didn't bother her nearly as much as it should have.

The heat, she told herself. It was so hot outside that she'd obviously suffered a minor heatstroke and so she wasn't thinking clearly. Because no way would she want anyone to know that their respectable leader had hooked up with the most disrespectable man in town.

The very last thing she needed was to tarnish her image. Unfortunately, what she needed and what she wanted were two very different things, and at that moment, the only thing she really wanted was Jesse.

In her bed and her life.

Temporarily, of course.

She knew full well that he was leaving in a few days, and she was staying, and that was that.

There would be no long-distance texts, no late-night phone calls, no keeping in touch. Jesse meant to let go of the past, to erase it, and she meant to let him.

Cold turkey.

It worked.

She knew firsthand and where she'd turned her back once before, she intended to let him turn his now. He needed to forget this place.

He deserved to forget.

Which meant she would let him go. She had to.

But not yet. Not just yet.

"I'M TELLING YOU, James Lee, the door is locked from the inside." Lora Tremayne's voice penetrated the frantic beat of Jesse's heart.

"But this door ain't got no lock on the inside, Miss Lora," came the deep voice of City Hall's lead maintenance man. "Maybe you aren't pushing it hard enough."

Jesse felt Gracie's body go tense and he knew she'd heard the speculation outside the door. He leaned back and saw the worry that leapt into her bright blue eyes.

"I pushed on it plenty hard," James Lee went on. "It's not locked, but it might be barricaded. Someone's definitely in there."

"Maybe it's Mabel Green," said another female

voice and Jesse knew the situation had attracted the attention of more than one of the women on hand for the monthly meeting and bake sale. "She's been on a no-carb diet for the past six months and it's made her batty. She probably saw all those goodies and went on a binge."

"Sarah Eckles is doing the same diet," another voice said. "It could be her."

"Maybe it's an animal. I get possums in my trash all the time. One of 'em could have crawled in a window."

"Maybe it's a raccoon."

"Maybe it's a zombie."

The voices joined in a loud back and forth as the doorknob jiggled and James Lee did his best to push open the door.

"We have to get out of here," Gracie started, but Jesse touched a finger to her lips.

"Wait here and don't come out until the coast is clear." He worked at the buttons on his jeans and then pulled on his shirt. A split second later, he kissed her quickly on the lips before turning toward the door.

He pulled open the door just as James Lee pushed. The man would have tumbled him backward, but Jesse was much younger and stronger. James Lee stumbled backward instead as Jesse stepped forward, slipped out the door and shut it firmly behind him.

"Afternoon, ladies," he said, giving Lora and the half dozen women that surrounded her a wink and a tip of his hat.

"Jesse Chisholm," Lora said, her face puckering up as if she'd just sucked on a lemon. "What in land's sake are you doing here?"

"I must have got lost on my way to the clerk's office."

"You mistook the kitchen for the clerk's office?" She didn't look convinced.

Meanwhile the whispers floated around the room.

"The clerk's office? Fat chance on that."

"Why, that man cain't be up to no good."

"The Chisholms don't know the meaning of the word *good.*"

"Somebody better count the brownies and pies."

"I'm selling some property," Jesse announced, as if that would kill the speculation. It wouldn't. His last name was Chisholm and nothing would ever change that. He knew as much and he'd come to terms with it, but he explained anyway because this wasn't about him. It was about Gracie. She was stuck in the room behind him and he wanted to give her a way out that didn't involve waltzing past these gossips. "I must have taken a wrong turn."

"Likely story," Lora snorted in the condescending way that had earned her the reputation as the most stuck-up bitch in the county.

He ignored the urge to tell her which way to go and how fast to get there. Instead, his ears perked to the sound of footsteps behind him. So soft that no one else would have heard unless they were listening.

A slide and a faint thud and then all was quiet.

No jiggle of the knob behind him. No creak of hinges.

Nothing because Gracie was heeding his words and not coming out until the coast was clear.

He ignored the crazy disappointment that twisted at his insides. It wasn't as if he wanted her to waltz out in front of God and everybody and tarnish the image she'd fought so hard to build.

At the same time, he couldn't shake the sudden urge to feel her hand on his arm, her warmth beside him, as she stepped up and declared to the world that she was here with him. For him.

"I'll just be on my way."

"I'll show you to the clerk's office," James Lee offered. "It's just down the hall." The man started forward, but Jesse wasn't budging until he had the entire entourage behind him.

"You sure you don't want to escort me out yourself?" He eyed Lora. "Just to make sure I don't overpower James, here, and come back to steal a peach cobbler."

"A smart-ass just like your father," she muttered, but she started after him anyway. As expected, the women followed and soon they were moving down the hallway toward the county clerk's office. When they reached the doorway, James turned.

"Show's over, ladies. There's a bake sale still going on out on the lawn that could use all of you, not to mention y'all got your meeting to get to." He motioned back down the hall. "Just get on about your business. I'll take care of things here."

"Make sure you do," Lora said, giving Jesse one last scathing look. He grinned and her frown deepened before she turned on the women. She rattled off new duties to them and they all disappeared through a nearby door that led to the front lawn.

"Sorry about that, Mr. Chisholm," James said once the women had disappeared. "Those busybodies don't think before they start running their mouths."

He winked. "Saw you ride in Houston last year. You were something."

"Thanks, James Lee."

"Had my granddaughters with me. Bought 'em each a shirt with your name on it. Tickled 'em pink, it did."

"That's mighty nice of you."

"Ain't nothing nice about it. I was hoping you might sign those shirts for me. It sure would mean a lot to the girls."

"Bring them by the training facility and I'd be happy to. In fact, bring the girls with you. They could watch a few sessions. I might have some rodeo passes sitting around, too, for the next event if you think they might like that."

The maintenance man grinned from ear to ear. "Boy, would they ever."

THE COAST WAS CLEAR.

Gracie gathered her courage, slipped out of the storage room, hurried through the kitchen and moved down the hallway toward the ladies' room at the far end.

She needed a few minutes to herself before she headed back out to the bake sale and the curious faces and the hot gossip that Jesse James Chisholm had been shoplifting brownies and cakes.

As if.

Jesse would never do such a thing, even if he had destroyed a few goodies in the name of some really hot sex.

Heat swamped her as she remembered the frosting on her nipple, followed by his lips. And his tongue. And...

Sheesh, it was hot in here.

She pushed inside the restroom, hit the lock button on the door and made her way to the sink. A second later, she splashed cold water on her face and tried to understand what had just happened.

She'd hopped up onto the table and had sex with Jesse James Chisholm just inches away from a very nosy group of constituents.

Even more, she'd liked it.

She liked him.

She ditched the last thought and focused on grabbing a wad of paper towels to blot at her face.

She didn't *like* him. *Like* involved a connection that went beyond the physical. It involved shared interests and mutual respect and admiration. It meant understanding someone's hopes and dreams and—

Okay, so she liked him. A little.

He was a strong, compassionate man. A man who put family first. Who went after what he wanted. A man with hopes and dreams and determination.

A man with a future that did not involve Lost Gun or her or what they'd just shared.

Before she could dwell on the suddenly depressing thought, her cell phone rang. She fished it out of her pocket and hit the Talk button.

"Hey, sis," Charlie's voice floated over the line. "What's up?"

"My sugar level." She reached for another paper towel and dabbed at the water running down her neck. "I'm up to my elbows in brownies and cookies."

"A bake sale?"

"Unfortunately."

"Sounds like a blast. Listen, I just wanted to make

sure you got my message about this weekend. I hate to cancel on you, but I've got a lot going right now and—"

"Sure." Why the hell was it still so hot in here?

"—I really don't have time to drive all the way to Lost Gun just to make homemade pizzas, even though they're like *the* best pizzas in the world and you're the best and—what did you just say?"

"We can do it some other time." Gracie blew out a deep breath and made a mental note to ask Trina to have James Lee check the main air conditioning unit. "Don't worry about it." She tossed the used paper towels and tried to ignore the rush of heat as she stared into the mirror and noticed that she'd missed one of the buttons on her shirt.

"You're not mad, are you?"

"Of course not."

"Yes, you are," Charlie insisted, obviously startled when Gracie didn't launch into a ten-minute lecture about how she'd bought all the pizza ingredients and pulled out the Monopoly board.

She would have. She would have reminded her sister about all the details and how much fun they would have being together, but suddenly the only thing she could think of was how hot it was and how she desperately needed to calm down and how she really needed to forget Jesse Chisholm.

And the fact that she liked him.

"You're mad and worried," Charlie went on, "but I'm not a little girl anymore. I know how to take care of myself. I won't be out late and I'll be super careful and—"

"I know you will. Call me later." She killed the connection before her sister could ask another question.

And then she concentrated on redoing her shirt and returning to the real world without thinking about Jesse Chisholm and the all-important fact that she couldn't wait to see him again.

15

HE WAS FRIGGIN' CRAZY.

That was the only explanation for the fact that the more Jesse James Chisholm touched Gracie Stone, the more he kissed her and slid deep, deep inside, the more he wanted to do it again and again and again.

Crazy, all right.

While he managed to get himself up and out of bed the morning after, it wasn't getting easier the way he'd expected. The way he'd hoped.

He stood beside the bed early Friday morning—four days after he'd first gotten her into his bed—and stared down at her luscious body spread out on his plain cotton sheets. Instead of the motel, they'd been keeping company in his apartment at the training facility. Away from prying eyes and the horde of reporters camped out at the motel.

He left the tack room and headed for the main corral. He had to give her up. He told himself that as he checked the feeding troughs. He had to give her up and forget about their time together and start thinking about the future. About Austin and his next ride and—

"Jesse!"

The name rang out and scattered his thoughts the minute he spotted the woman on the opposite side of the railing.

"Hey there, Wendy." He climbed over the railing and headed around to where she stood. "Pete's not here. I dropped him off on your doorstep myself last night after the bachelor party."

"I know, and thanks for not getting too wild and crazy. He said you kept it low-key."

He hadn't meant to. He'd meant to take Pete over to Luscious Longhorns and get them both as drunk as skunks. But Pete had been more interested in texting Wendy and Jesse had been more interested in getting back to Gracie, and so they'd left Cole and Billy and Jimmy and Jake to tie one on and close the place down.

"I'm not looking for Pete," she went on. "I'm looking for you. I need a favor."

"I really need to get going. I promised Eli I'd—"

"It's my cousin. She's flying in for the wedding this afternoon and I need someone to pick her up."

"I'll get one of the boys to drive out—"

"And take her to the wedding. And keep her company."

"I'm sure Joe or Sam or—"

"I need you, Jesse. I was thinking you could be her date for the wedding."

"But I already have a date."

"You do?"

That's right, buddy. You do?

Okay, so he didn't actually have a date, but he wanted one. He wanted to ask Gracie to be his date. The thing was, he wasn't one hundred percent positive she would say yes. When it came to sex, he knew she couldn't resist him. But this was different. This wasn't about being lovers. It was about being companions. Friends. And to a man who'd been judged and shunned most of his life, those were much harder to come by. Gracie had called it quits and turned her back on him once before. He wasn't going to be blindsided again.

"It's not one of the Barbies, is it?" Wendy went on. "I know they're a lot of fun, but I thought you might want to meet someone with a little substance. Someone more long term—"

"Okay, I'll do it." He planted a kiss on her cheek. "Text me the flight information and I'll see to it she gets to the motel in one piece. And the wedding." And then he turned and walked away before he did something really stupid—like change his mind.

Gracie wasn't dating material. What they had was purely physical and very, very temporary. She'd made that clear from the get-go. Not that he wanted anything more permanent. Hell, he was leaving in two days. No strings. No regrets.

That meant ignoring the feelings churning deep in his gut and laying the past to rest once and for all.

He wasn't falling for her all over again.

Not this time.

Never, ever again.

THE WOMAN WAS driving him to drink.

Jesse finished off the last of his second beer and reached for number three as he watched Gracie two-step around the dance floor with one of Pete's ranch hands. Even dressed in a plain beige skirt and a matching jacket that did nothing to accent the luscious curves hidden beneath, she looked good enough to eat. With every turn, the skirt pulled and tugged across her round ass. With every dip, the bodice of her jacket shifted and he glimpsed the full swells of her breasts. A thin line of perspiration dotted her forehead, making her face glow. Her lips were full and pink and parted in a smile—

Hell's bells, she was smiling at the two-bit cowboy. She wasn't supposed to be doing that. She wasn't even supposed to be here. Her name hadn't been anywhere near the guest list and so he'd been more than a little shocked when she'd waltzed up to him, flashed a press pass, snapped a picture and said, "June Silsbee, the about-town photographer for the newspaper, is sick. I'm filling in for her."

Only she wasn't standing around on the fringes, snapping pictures for the world to see. No, she was having fun. Dancing. Laughing. *Smiling.*

Jesse latched onto beer number four as the song played down and Gracie traded Pete's ranch hand and the two-step for Eli and a popular line dance.

She twirled and wiggled her ass and smiled—holy crap, there she was smiling again. And winking. And at a man old enough to be her father.

Not that Jesse had any room to talk. He'd let Wendy fix him up with the brunette sitting next to him. A mistake if he'd ever made one. While she was nice enough, she wasn't Gracie.

And the problem is?

No problem, he told himself for the umpteenth time, shifting his attention to the woman and trying to focus on whatever she was saying. Something about the bridesmaids' dresses and how pretty everything had been and what a great time she was having.

"Would you excuse me for just a second?" A few seconds later, he left Lisa or Lynette or whatever her name was staring after him as he headed for the bar and did his damnedest to ignore the sexy blonde who floated around the dance floor.

"Beer?" the bartender asked, but Jesse shook his head.

"I need something stronger." A split second later the man pulled a jar of clear liquid from behind the bar and held it up. Jesse nodded and reached for the homemade moonshine.

He was on swig number three when Billy cut in for a waltz with Gracie. Jesse's hands tightened on the jar and he fought the urge to rush over, pull Gracie into his arms and make her smile and wink at him. An urge he managed to resist until Billy closed the few inches that separated them. Jesse forgot all about his moonshine.

"Don't you have your own date?" He tapped his brother on the shoulder. "Shouldn't you be dancing with her?"

"Are you kidding?" He motioned to Casey Jessup, who sat near the bar, her elbow planted on top, her entire focus on the man she was currently arm-wrestling. "She hates to dance."

"So go referee the match for her." He elbowed his way in between them, his gaze fixed on the surprised woman who stared back at him.

"Don't you have your own date?" Gracie arched an eyebrow as he pulled her close.

"It's not an official date. I'm just keeping her company for Wendy."

"You're doing a piss-poor job considering you're here with me."

"I want to dance." He slid a possessive arm around her waist and pulled her close.

"What's gotten into you?"

"A special batch of white lightning."

She pulled back. "Big Earl's white lightning?"

"Something like that." His gaze caught and held hers. "You look really nice."

"You're drunk."

"Not drunk enough. I don't like it when you dance with other men."

"Then you should have asked me to be your date instead of bringing someone else."

"It's not a date."

"It sure looks like a date."

"You're right. I'm sorry." He stared deep into her eyes. "I should have asked you to come with me, but I didn't. I thought I needed some distance. But it doesn't matter if you're clear across the room or right next to me, I still want you the same." He saw the flash of surprise in her gaze. "I need you." He pressed a kiss to her soft lips before pulling her close. She seemed stiff at first, as if she didn't believe him. But then just like that, her body seemed to relax. She inched closer. And the rest of the world faded and they started to dance.

GRACIE HAD WON the battle, but not the war, she realized later that night when she rolled over after several hours of Jesse's fast and furious lovemaking to find the bed next to her warm but empty. As usual. Instead of the motel, he'd taken her to the training facility and the comfy full-size bed that filled up the bedroom of the small apartment that sat over his office. She heard him moving around in the next room—the creak of the chair as he yanked on his boots, the slide of change as he loaded hi' pockets, the clink of a coffee cup as he finished his last swallow. He was leaving her again. It was still dark, still a long way until sunrise, and Jesse was heading out to practice the way he had last night and the night before.

Admiration crept through her, along with a surge of anxiety. This was it. It was well past midnight, which meant that Saturday had come and gone and it was officially Sunday morning. The wedding was over and there was nothing keeping Jesse in Lost Gun. He would pick up and head for Austin first thing tomorrow morning. Even more, she would take her oath of office and assume the role of mayor.

It was now or never. Otherwise, she would never really know if she'd meant more to him than just a casual fling. If after today he would at least think about her every now and then. Remember her. And she would remember him. She pulled on his tuxedo shirt, snatched up the camera she'd been using at the wedding and started for the adjoining room. She wanted, needed, a place in Jesse Chisholm's memory since she couldn't claim a place in his heart.

JESSE HAD JUST retrieved a blanket from the tack room and walked back to the corral when the gate creaked open and he heard the camera click.

His entire body went on high alert when he caught sight of her—her long blond hair tousled, her face soft and flushed from sleep, her lips swollen from his kisses. She clasped her camera in one hand and a pang of nostalgia went through him. She wore only his white tuxedo shirt and an old worn pair of his boots. The shirt stopped mid-thigh, revealing long, sexy-as-hell legs. He felt a stir in his groin despite the fact that he should have had his fill of her by now.

He was full. Sated. Sick.

That was what he told himself, but damned if he felt it as she walked into the barn. The tuxedo shirt, unbuttoned to reveal the swell of her luscious breasts, teased him with each step. She snapped a few more pictures of him, the *click, click, click* keeping time with the sudden beat of his heart.

Work, he told himself, forcing his gaze away, determined to get back to work. He headed for the mechanical bull sitting off to the side of the rodeo arena where he'd been adjusting the settings. He leaned down and reached up under the backside of the bull to change the speed and friction. Harder. Faster. That's what he needed right now.

Unfortunately, *harder* and *faster* weren't the two words to be thinking of at the moment. Not with her so close.

He felt her gaze and every nerve in his body cracked to attention. He frowned. He was in the homestretch. No more wanting what he couldn't have. No more Gracie.

As relieved as the thought should have made him, the only thing he felt at that moment was desperation. To get back to work, he reminded himself. He was desperate to get the hell out of Lost Gun and head to Austin. End of story.

"What are you doing out here?" he asked gruffly.

"Same as you." She hooked her camera over a nearby corral post. Boots crunched as she neared the mechanical bull. "I thought I'd take a ride."

The words drew his gaze and he found her standing on the opposite side of the bull. "I hate to break it to you, sugar, but you can't ride."

"Maybe not at this moment, but practice makes perfect." Her eyes glittered. Her full lips curved into a half smile that did funny things to his heartbeat. "This is a training facility, right?"

"Last time I looked."

"So train me." She gripped the saddle horn, swung a sexy leg over and mounted up. "I'm all yours."

If only.

He shook away the thought and swallowed against the sudden tightness in his throat. "You're serious?"

"As serious as Old Lady Mitchell's last heart attack."

He eyed her for a moment more before he shrugged. "All right, then." He motioned to the side. "Put your right hand in the grip."

She slid her fingers under the leather strap. "What next?"

"Put your left up in the air."

"Okay."

"Now arch your back."

She thrust her breasts forward and an invisible fist punched in right in the sternum. "What now?"

He drew in some much needed air and tried to keep his voice calm. "Hold on tight."

He flipped the switch and the bull started to rock back and forth, this way and that.

"Mmm…" She closed her eyes at the subtle motion and a smile touched her lips. "Now I know why you cowboys spend so much time doing this."

"I don't think it's the same for us cowboys. Different parts."

Her eyes snapped open then and her passion-filled gaze met his. "I know." The bull kept moving and her eyelids drifted shut again. She threw her head back, her eyes closed, her lips parted as she leaned back and rocked her lower body, following the motion of the bull.

A sight that shouldn't affect him. After a week together, she was out of his system. His head was on straight, his mind back on business, his future crystal clear.

A soft, familiar sigh quivered in the air and the sound sent a bolt of need through him. A wave of possessiveness rolled through him and burned away reason. He flipped the switch and the bull slowed to a halt. He closed the distance between them in a few quick steps.

At the first touch of his fingertips on her thigh, her eyes fluttered open.

She stared down at him, her eyes bright and feverish. "Is it over already?"

"It's just getting started." He reached across her lap and urged her other leg over the bull until she sat sideways, facing him, her lap level with his shoulders. "*I'm* just getting started." He shoved the shirt up and spread her legs wide, wedging his shoulders between her knees. "Ah, baby, you're a natural." Her slick folds were pink and swollen after her recent ride, and he knew she was close. "You've got perfect form." He touched her, trailed a fingertip over the hot, moist flesh and relished the moan that vibrated from her lips. "So damned perfect."

There were no more words after that. He hooked her booted ankles over his shoulders, tilted her body a fraction just to give him better access, dipped his head and tasted her sweetness.

She cried out at the first lap of his tongue and threaded her fingers through his hair to hold him close. But he wasn't going anywhere. This was her first time on the back of a mechanical bull and Jesse intended to make it the wildest, most memorable ride of her life.

He devoured her, licking and sucking and nibbling, pushing her higher and higher and, oddly enough, climbing right along with her. He took his own pleasure by pleasuring her and when she screamed his name and came apart in his arms, the feelings that rushed through him—the triumph and the satisfaction and the warmth—felt as good as any orgasm he'd ever had.

Chemistry, a voice whispered. They were simply good together. That explained her effect on him.

It wasn't because she was different.

Because she was his one and only.

That's what he wanted to think. But truthfully, he didn't just want to hoist her over his shoulder, take her back to the bed and drive deep, deep inside her deliciously hot body until he reached his own climax.

He wanted to curl up with her afterward, talk to her, laugh with her, hold her. He wanted to walk down Main Street, her hand in his, and let the world know that she was his. She always had been.

She always would be.

Need gripped him, fierce and demanding and intense. He gathered her in his arms and started for the office.

"What about your training?" she murmured against his neck.

"It'll wait."

THE MINUTE JESSE pressed her down on the bed, Gracie knew something had changed. There was an urgency, a fierceness about him that she'd never seen before. Tension held his body tight, every muscle taut. His hands felt strong and purposeful and desperate as he ripped off his clothes, spread her legs wide and slid home in one fierce thrust.

"You are the wildest woman," he growled, resting his forehead against hers for several fast, furious heartbeats. "My woman."

She didn't expect the declaration any more than the determination that glittered in his eyes as he stared down at her, into her. And she certainly didn't anticipate the pure joy that rushed through her.

Before she could dwell on the feeling, large hands gripped her buttocks and tilted. He slid a fraction deeper and all rational thought fled.

The next few moments passed in a frenzy of need as Jesse pumped into her over and over, as if his life depended on every deep, penetrating thrust. His mouth ate at hers, and his touch was greedy and hungry, as if he could no longer control his need for her. As if he'd stopped trying. They joined together on a basic, primitive level unlike anything she'd ever experienced before, and as she stared up into his face at his fierce, wild expression, she knew she'd driven him over the edge. Way, way over.

The realization sent a thrill coursing through her, followed by warning bells. But before she could worry over what the change meant, he slid his hand between them and touched her where they joined, and she went wild with him.

Seconds later she screamed his name for the second time that morning as her climax slammed into her and she shattered in his arms. Another fierce pounding thrust, and Jesse followed her into oblivion, her name bursting from his lips as he spilled himself deep.

"I love you," he groaned as he collapsed atop her, his arms solid and warm, his body pressing her into the mattress.

I love you.

The words echoed through her head and sent a swell of happiness through her for a full moment before Gracie remembered the last thing, the very last thing, she wanted from Jesse James Chisholm was his love.

Love? He couldn't... He wouldn't... No! This wasn't happening. Not him and her and *love*.

"I really have to go." She scrambled from the bed, her heart pounding furiously as she snatched up her clothes in record time. She retrieved her camera from the corral and then Gracie did what any responsible, dedicated community leader would do with a totally inappropriate, sexy cowboy who loved her right at her fingertips.

She ran for her life.

JESSE LISTENED TO Gracie's footsteps as she left the training facility and barely resisted the urge to go after her. He wanted to. He wanted to haul ass, toss her over his shoulder and keep her here forever. *She was his.*

Now and always.

But the thing was, she wasn't his. Not now. And, judging by the panicked expression on her face when he'd declared his feelings, *always* seemed pretty far out of the question, too.

Not that she didn't have feelings for him. She did.

She felt the same chemistry. The undeniable attraction. Even the companionship that came with being friends at one time and sharing a history. But love?

Maybe.

But if she did, it wasn't going to matter. She'd learned to put her feelings second, behind everything and everyone else in her life. She had too many people depending on her, watching her, judging her.

He knew the feeling.

He'd spent a lifetime being the object of everyone's scrutiny. Hell, he still was. Being escorted out of a bake sale, of all things, proved as much. It testified to the fact that there were folks in town who had no intention of forgetting who he was or what his father had done.

And James Lee and his granddaughters proved there were a few who couldn't care less about Jesse's past. A few who accepted him for who he was and what he'd done with his own life. Like Wanda Loftis who worked at the local pizza parlor. Wanda always gave him extra cheese on his pepperoni. A celebrity perk, she'd told him time and time again when he'd offered to pay, only she'd always given him extra cheese even way back when he'd been barely able to scrape together enough money to pay for a small to share with his brothers. And there was Mason Connor, the local pharmacist who'd given him free antibiotic samples that one time when Billy had caught strep back in kindergarten. And Miss Laura, the head waitress at the diner, who had his coffee and a great big smile waiting for him the minute he walked in on Saturday mornings. She'd given him leftovers too many times to count back when his daddy had been alive and food had been scarce. She'd helped him then, and she still had a smile for him when she spotted him now.

The realization sent a rush of warmth through him even though he'd learned a long time ago that the only opinion that really mattered at the end of the day was his own. It was nice to know he had a few supporters in Lost Gun. Friends even.

Which explains why you're still running away.

The minute the thought struck, he tried to push it back out. He wasn't running from anything. He was burying the past. Making peace. Moving on.

Running.

The truth struck, sticking in his head as he pulled on his clothes, parked his hat on top of his head, and headed outside to his pickup truck.

It was just this side of seven a.m. and he needed to get a move on. He had a meeting with Eli to tie up all the loose ends at the training facility—he'd sold all of his stock except for his one new bull and he needed to make arrangements for the old cowboy to look after it until he made arrangements for transport. That, and he needed to pick up the last few boxes of his stuff still stashed at Pete's ranch. Afterwards, he was going to head back into Lost Gun and swing by the motel to say goodbye to his brothers. Then it was just a matter of pointing his truck toward the city limits, pressing on the gas and getting the hell out of Dodge.

Once and for all.

He climbed behind the wheel and gunned the engine. It was the first morning of the rest of his life free and clear of his past. His lawyer had several prospective buyers on the list for his dad's run-down property. Hell, one of them had even made an offer. A damned nice one. Plenty for him to take his share and invest in his very own training facility closer to his spread in Austin. Maybe even buy one clear and outright for himself. Then when his heyday ended as PBR's number one, he could stop riding and start coaching the up-and-comers. That, or breed his own bucking bulls. He'd entertained that possibility, as well.

Either way, he had a solid plan.

One that had kept him up thinking and planning and dreaming on so many lonely nights.

It just didn't fill him with the same sense of hope that it once had. There was no rush of excitement. No sense of accomplishment. No flash of impatience to haul ass and never look back.

Instead, Jesse spent the next half hour driving out to the Gunner spread at a slow crawl that had even Martin Keyhole—the ninety-five-year-old owner of a nearby turtle farm—lying on his horn. Sure, Jesse tried to oblige and pick up his speed, but damned if his boot would stay down. There was just too much going on his head.

Because as much as he wanted to, he couldn't stop thinking about Gracie and the town, and the undeniable truth that whether he went after his own training facility or started breeding his own bucking bulls, he could do either of them right here. Even more, he couldn't shake the feeling that if he did leave, he would be running away from the best thing that had ever happened to him.

16

GRACIE PULLED OUT onto Main Street and took a whopping bite of the extra large fudge brownie she'd just picked up at the local bakery. Her second in less than fifteen minutes. She'd scarfed number one after three cups of coffee and a carob-covered scone from The Green Machine which had done nothing to touch the hunger that ate away inside of her. So she'd caved and walked into the bakery where she'd spent fifteen minutes listening to the clerk, Marjorie Wilbur, complain yet again about the pothole on the corner of Main and Hill Country before taking the rest of her order to go.

She hung a left at the first corner and waited for the rush of satisfaction that always came with even the smallest nibble of her favorite dessert, and the guilt. Especially the guilt. Anything to escape the feelings still pushing and pulling inside of her thanks to Jesse and his declaration.

The heat of the moment.

That's all it had been. Guys were notorious for it and so it should have come as no surprise. Hell, it was a wonder he hadn't proposed after the way she'd rocked his world.

That's what she told herself as she stuffed another bite into her mouth and tried to lose herself in the rich taste of chocolate and the all-important fact that she'd fallen off the wagon in a major way. Not one, but two brownies. She was a loser. A slug. She should feel terrible.

Not excited.

Or happy.

Or anxious to head back to the training facility, throw herself into Jesse's arms and beg him to take her away with him.

Yeah, right.

She hung a left at the second stop sign and eased onto her street. She had a life here with potholes to fix and a town that depended on her and a sister who needed her.

The minute the thought struck, she noted the familiar red Prius parked in her driveway. Charlie was home.

And Gracie wasn't.

She stifled a wave of guilt and pulled into the driveway. Stuffing the bakery bag under her seat, she snagged the camera and her purse and climbed out of the car.

"I thought you weren't coming home this weekend," she said when she walked into the living room to find her younger sister sitting cross-legged on the couch, her laptop balanced on her knees. The petite blonde, hair pulled back in a loose ponytail, wore a Texas Longhorns T-shirt, a pair of sweats and an expression that said *you are so busted.* "I would have had the blueberry pancakes ready and waiting had I known—"

"I'm not eating pancakes anymore," Charlie cut

in. "Too much processed flour. And I wasn't coming home this weekend. But you sounded funny when I last talked to you, so I got worried." She shrugged. "I drove in last night."

"*You* were worried about *me?*"

"You didn't sound like your usual neurotic self when I told you I wasn't coming home. No twenty questions about where I was going or what I was doing. No blasting me about being careful. I figured you were sick, but I'm starting to think it might be something else. Or someone else." A knowing light gleamed in her gaze. "You've been out all night."

"I was working late."

"I drove by City Hall. I didn't see your car."

"I wasn't at City Hall. I was at the Gunner ranch. I was helping out with the local newspaper. Their photographer is out, so I offered to take pictures at Pete's wedding for the About Town section."

Charlie didn't look convinced. "That would put you home at midnight."

"I wasn't tired so I drove over to the all-night movie festival in Milburn county."

"All-night movies, huh?" Charlie's fingers moved across the laptop keyboard for a few frantic heartbeats before her gaze narrowed. "The only all-night movie festival in Milburn is Kung Fu Movie Madness at the Palladium." She eyed Gracie. "Since when did you become a Bruce Lee fan?"

"Are you kidding? I love Bruce Lee." Gracie sat her purse aside and headed for the kitchen. "He's super athletic. Listen, I've got some fresh fruit if you're hungry...." Her words trailed off as she headed straight for the refrigerator and tried to ignore the rush of guilt.

"And since when do you take pictures?" Charlie shifted the subject back to the wedding as she followed Gracie into the kitchen. "You don't even own a camera anymore."

"Yes, I do. I just don't use it."

Charlie gave her a knowing look. "Something's up with you."

"Nothing's up." Gracie ignored the gleam in her sister's eyes and busied herself pulling several peaches and a crate of strawberries from the refrigerator. "I was just helping out. It's my job. I'm trying to beef up my public service presence before the inauguration. Speaking of which, I was planning on getting a new dress, so maybe we can go shopping next weekend—"

"It's okay, you know." Charlie leaned on the granite countertop and plucked a ripe strawberry from the container. "It's high time you got a life."

"I have a life, thank you very much." Gracie retrieved a container of yogurt.

"No, you don't." Charlie nibbled on the ripe red fruit. "You facilitate everyone else's life."

"I'm the mayor." Gracie set the yogurt on the counter and reached for two bowls in a nearby cabinet. "That's what I do."

"No, you're you." Charlie pointed the strawberry at her. "That's what *you* do. You make sure everyone else is happy and healthy, but you don't waste five minutes worrying over yourself." The words hung between them for a long moment before her sister added, "You deserve to be happy and healthy, too, you know."

"I am happy." And healthy. Or she had been before Jesse's impromptu declaration and the double dose of brownies. "I'm happy if you're happy."

"That's the thing." Charlie abandoned the half-eaten strawberry. "I have enough stress. Do you know how much pressure I deal with knowing that your well-being rests on my shoulders?"

Gracie thought of the past twelve years since her brother's death. "Actually, I do."

"Then you know it's not that much fun." A pleading note crept into her voice. "I was supposed to go with Aubry and Sue to Dallas to go club-hopping, but I bailed on them to drive here because I was worried about you."

"I wish you wouldn't have done that."

"I did it because I know you would do the same for me. I know you love me, Gracie. You don't have to keep trying to prove it."

"I just want you to feel it. Every second of every day. I want to be there for you—"

"That's the thing," she cut in, "you can't. Not all the time. Not because you don't love me, but because that's the way life is. It's a bitch sometimes and there are moments when things don't always pan out. I'm going to have to stand on my own two feet eventually. All by myself. Alone. That doesn't mean I'm lonely, but you are. Which is why I was thinking that we could sign you up for one of those online dating sites. A friend of mine's mother did it and she has a date every Saturday night—"

"Charlie, I'm not lonely."

"You went to an all-night Bruce Lee festival," Charlie pointed out. "You're beyond lonely. You're just this side of depraved. You need a man."

"Just because I don't have a man doesn't mean I'm lonely or depraved. I've got an entire town to keep me company." She eyed the dog wagging at her feet. "And Sugar, too."

Charlie bent down and picked up the ball of fluff. She gave the animal an affectionate scratch behind the ears. "You really think Sugar Lips, here, is a fitting substitute for a *man?*"

She thought of Jesse and the past few nights they'd spent together. She remembered the way he'd touched her and kissed her and laughed when she'd said something really funny. The way he'd looked at her when she'd talked about her past, as if he understood what she felt. As if he felt it, too.

And then she thought of the nights that lay ahead with Sugar curled up on her lap and the remote control in her hand and the latest reality show blaring on the TV.

"Which dating site was that?" she heard herself ask.

Gracie spent Sunday morning trying not to think about Jesse. Or the all-important fact that he loved her and she loved him and he was still leaving. He hadn't said a word otherwise. No phone call. No text. Nothing but silence.

Not that it would have made a difference. She'd made her choice. Her life was here.

Which was why she'd dragged herself into City Hall to get a jump-start on her week. She had dozens of things to do before the inauguration in one week. Today alone she had to put in an appearance at the local tractor races, recite the Pledge of Allegiance at the weekly softball games and then dish up potato salad for the afternoon picnic at the Lost Gun Presbyterian Church. Even if she wasn't too keen on facing an entire town

full of people at the moment. She would do it anyway—
all of it—because it was her duty. Gracie had made a
promise, and she always kept her promises. *Always*.

But first…

She focused on the lime-green Hula-Hoop in her
hands and started to swirl her hips. A quick twist of
the hoop and for the next few seconds, she moved in
perfect synchronization with the plastic circle swirling
around her waist. But then it fell and she found herself
back at square one.

"Why are you doing this?" Trina asked when she
walked into Gracie's office to find her huffing and
puffing and sweating up a storm.

"Because I promised Sue Ann Miller that I would do
the Hula-Hoop for Hope with the rest of her Brownie
troop tomorrow afternoon. I won't buy much hope if
I can't Hula-Hoop for more than ten seconds a pop.
People pledge by the minute."

"I'm not talking about the Hula-Hoop. I'm talking about this." She motioned at the office surrounding them. "All of this. It's Sunday. A day of rest. You
should be sitting in your backyard, sipping a mai tai
and reading a romance novel or a glamour mag. Or
traipsing through the woods with that camera you love
so much."

"I don't use my camera anymore."

"Sure, you don't." Her eyes twinkled. "I saw you
last night at the wedding. The entire town saw you."

"That's different." She remembered all of the pics
of Jesse she'd snapped at the training facility after the
festivities. Pics that had nothing to do with what was
happening about town and everything to do with the
fact that she'd wanted to keep him with her. Not that

she was admitting as much to Trina. "I was filling in for June."

"You were enjoying yourself, which is what you should be doing right now. Instead, you're working. You're cooped up when you hate being cooped up. You hate going to city council meetings and old-lady breakfasts and monthly VFW luncheons."

"I don't hate it."

"You don't like it."

"I'm good at it."

"That's not the point. Aren't you tired of faking it?" Trina echoed the one question that had been nagging at her all morning.

She *did* hate playing the part of little Miss Perfect. Sure, she was good at it. She'd learned to be good at it, but she didn't actually *like* it.

She never had and she never would.

"It doesn't matter what I like or what I don't like. I'm still the mayor-elect."

"And as mayor-elect, you are more than capable of picking a replacement should you decide to retire early."

The meaning of Trina's words sank in and for the first time in a very long time, Gracie felt a flutter of excitement deep inside.

"I can't just give it all up." That was what she said, but where that statement had been true twelve years ago, it was no longer true now. Times had changed. *She'd* changed. She didn't have to keep playing the martyr. She knew that.

At the same time, she'd been doing it for so long that she wasn't so sure she could stop. Even if she desperately wanted to.

An image of Jesse pushed into her head and she remembered the possessive look on his face when he'd cut in to dance with her last night. He'd taken her into his arms and held her as if he never meant to let her go.

He'd also been tipsy thanks to the primo moonshine that had been circulating at last night's wedding.

She ignored the ache in her chest and focused on doing something—anything—to keep her mind off Jesse and the fact that he was leaving and she was letting him go. Without putting up a fight. Or telling him how she felt.

"Where are you going?" Trina asked when Gracie abandoned the Hula-Hoop and reached for her purse.

"I need to see a man about some moonshine."

"You really think Big Earl is cooking again?"

Gracie thought of the pint of white lightning she'd seen at the wedding the night before and then she thought of the way Casey Jessup had helped her great-grandfather into his chair. "I think it's his recipe, but I don't think he's the one doing the cooking."

Gracie's instincts were jumping and buzzing because she knew Casey had something to do with the case of white lightning at the wedding the night before. It was just a matter of proving it.

"My great-grandpa's taking a nap. You'll have to come back later," Casey said when Gracie knocked on the door a half hour later, after another visit to the butcher.

"I'm not here to talk to him." She glanced behind her at the dogs busy devouring the raw meat before turning a pleading look on Casey. "I want to talk to you and I'd like to do it with all of my limbs intact."

Casey looked undecided for a split second before she shrugged and stepped aside.

Gracie retreated into the safety of the double-wide trailer. A faint snore drifted from a nearby bedroom, confirming that Casey, at least, wasn't lying about Big Earl's nap.

"I know you made the moonshine for him," Gracie said, turning on the young woman. "I also know that you aren't going to do it again—otherwise I'll be obliged to report you to the sheriff."

Casey looked as if she wanted to deny the accusation, but then she shrugged. "It's no big deal. It was just one batch."

"It's still illegal."

The girl glanced toward the open bedroom door. "But cooking makes him happy, and not much else does these days. He used to love his crosswords, but now he can't see the puzzle. And he used to love to watch his old Western flicks, but now he can't even do that because of his glaucoma. And he cain't cook either and enjoy a glass every night like he used to on account of he can't see or move around or do anything else like he used to. So I took his recipe and I did it myself so he wouldn't miss out on the one thing he can do, and that's drink. I just want him to be happy."

Enough to sacrifice her own freedom should she gt caught.

Gracie knew the feeling.

"I understand you did it for a good reason, but it's still highly illegal. You can't cook out here. He'll have to switch to beer or whiskey or something they actually sell in a store."

"And if he doesn't?"

"Then I'll have the sheriff arrest the both of you. Consider this your warning. No more cooking."

Casey nodded and Gracie knew she'd won this battle. But Big Earl was well over ninety years old and had acquired a taste for moonshine a long, long time ago. Even more, Casey was too devoted to deny the old man much of anything. And so Gracie wasn't so sure she was going to win this war.

Still, she intended to try.

"No cooking," she said again, and then she held her breath, darted out the door and raced for her car.

A HALF HOUR later Trina was on her fourth drink while Gracie worked on her second. They sat at a small table at a local sports bar that was all but deserted thanks to the softball game going on down at the ball field. Still, a few die-hard football fans sat in the far corner, as well as the entire ladies' sewing circle who were drinking peach schnapps and watching a rerun of *Bridezillas* on one of the monstrous TV screens.

Gracie's gaze swiveled away from a bitchy bride named Soleil just in time to see a pair of worn jeans moving toward her. Her gaze slid higher, over trim thighs and a lean waist, to a faded denim shirt covering a broad chest… Jesse. A straw Resistol sat atop his dark head, slanted at just the angle she remembered and making him look every bit the cowboy who'd stolen her heart.

"Shouldn't you be on the interstate by now?" she asked as he stopped next to her table.

"I forgot something." Jesse's gaze caught and held hers and his words echoed in her head.

"What?"

"You."

Joy erupted inside her, stirring a wave of panic that made her heart pound faster.

"I don't know what you mean."

"I want you to come with me." His gaze darkened. "Be with me. You don't belong here, Gracie. You and I both know that."

"You don't know anything. Sorry, Trina," she told her assistant as she pushed to her feet. "I need to get out of here." Before Jesse could reach for her, she started past him toward the nearest exit. Fear pushed her faster when she heard Jesse's voice behind her.

"Gracie, wait!"

But she couldn't. Not because he wanted her to go but because she wanted it. She wanted to chuck it all, throw herself into his arms, walk away and never look back. The knowledge sent a rush of anxiety through her and she picked up her steps. She slammed her palms against the exit door and stumbled out into the parking lot. Gravel crunched as her legs ate up the distance to the car.

"Gracie!" The name rang out a second before he caught her arm in a firm jerk that brought her whirling around to face him. "Gracie, I—"

"Don't say it!" She shook her head, blinking back the tears that suddenly threatened to overwhelm her. "Please don't say it again."

"I love you."

The tears spilled over and she shook her head, fighting the truth of his words and the emotion in her heart. "Let me go. I—I need to get back to the office. I've got work to do."

"Gracie?" Strong, warm hands cradled her face, his

thumbs smoothing her tears. "What is it, baby? Didn't you hear me? You know I love—"

"Don't!" Pleasure rushed through her, so fierce it stirred the fear and the panic and made her fight harder. She pushed at his hands. "Don't say those things to me. Don't make this situation any harder. You have to leave and I have to let you."

"If saying I love you makes it harder for you to let me go, then I love you, I love you, I will *always* love you." His eyes took on a determined light. "That's why I want you to come with me. I thought you'd be happy. I thought you wanted out of this town."

"You thought wrong."

"Did I?" His fierce violet gaze held hers, coaxing and tempting, and she came so close to throwing herself into his arms—to hell with Lost Gun.

Instead, she shook her head, clinging to her anger and her fear and the pain of hearing her sister cry herself to sleep every night after their brother passed away. Charlie had been so uncertain for so long, but Gracie had changed all of that. *She'd* changed.

While she wasn't the goody-goody she pretended to be and she was far from content, she still liked it here. She liked the people and the town and her house.

Her home.

"I'm not going with you. I made a commitment to the people of this town. I have a responsibility. I can't drop everything just because you say you love me."

"How about because *you* love *me?*"

She shook her head. "I don't. I can't."

No matter how much she wanted to.

She fought against the emotion that gripped her heart and made her want to throw all pride aside, wrap her arms around him and confess the feelings welling inside of her.

"It doesn't matter how we feel. It doesn't change the fact that you have to go and I have to stay. I *have* to." She yanked free and started for her car, steps echoing in her head like a death knell. Inside, she gunned the engine and took a deep, shaking breath.

Heaven help her, she'd done it. She'd done the right thing by giving Jesse the freedom he so desperately needed.

So why did it suddenly feel as if Gracie had turned her back on the one thing that mattered most?

Wiping frantically at a flood of hot tears, she chanced a glance in her mirror to see Jesse standing where she'd left him, staring after her, fists clenched, his body taut, as if it took all his strength not to go after her.

It was an image that haunted her all through the night and the rest of the week as Gracie wrote her acceptance speech and picked out a dress for the inauguration and prepared for the rest of her life.

Without Jesse Chisholm.

"Let her loose!" Jesse yelled, stuffing his hand beneath the rope and holding on for all he was worth. The two cowboys monitoring the chute threw open the doors. The bull reared and darted forward, nearly throwing Jesse, who held tight, riding the fledgling for the very first time.

He held on, his grip determined as the bull kicked and stomped and snorted against the feel of the weight on his back. Seconds ticked by as he bucked and twisted and made Jesse the proud papa of a brand-new bucking bull.

Cheers went up a few minutes later as he climbed off after a brief but exhilarating ride.

"You did good, boy," he murmured, wishing Pete could have been there. But he was off on his honeymoon with Wendy, making memories and babies.

A pang of envy shot through Jesse. While he'd achieved so much in his life, he was just getting started. He had years left on the circuit. Too long to be thinking about a future beyond.

A home. Kids. Gracie.

It was three days since he'd last seen her. Instead of hauling ass to Austin on Sunday, he'd gone back to the Gunner ranch to pick up some boxes and ended up staying the night. To think on things and try to get his head on straight. Then Monday had rolled around and his lawyer had called with two more buyers and Jesse had stayed to meet with the man and go over things later that day. And then Tuesday had rolled around and he'd had papers to sign. And Wednesday he'd had to accept delivery of the fledgling bull since Eli had made an appointment to get new glasses.

But tomorrow… Tomorrow was the day.

Jesse helped the hands get Ranger back into his chute. He'd just flipped the latch when he caught sight of a familiar car pulling into the parking lot.

He pulled off his gloves, exited the corral and started toward her. Gracie climbed out of the car and met him near the front entrance.

"You're here," he said, his heart pitching and shaking faster than a bull busting out of the chute.

"I heard you got delayed with the offers on your

place and so I thought I'd stop by before you finally do hit the road." She handed him a box. "I made it for you. Something to remember me by."

As if he could forget her.

She'd lived and breathed in his memories for so long and now she'd taken up permanent residence in his heart, and there wasn't a damn thing he could do about it.

There was, a nagging voice whispered. He could hitch her over his shoulder, load her into his pickup truck and haul ass for Austin. And when he got there, he could love her until she changed her mind and stayed. The heat burned so fierce between them it would be hot enough to change her mind. For a little while, anyway.

But then she would leave. He knew it. She belonged here and he didn't, and there wasn't a damned thing he could do about it.

His fingers itched and he touched her hand. Her gaze met his and he read the fear in her eyes, the uncertainty. As much as she wanted him to stay, she wanted to go. But she was afraid. Afraid to follow, to abandon the town that had embraced her when she'd needed them.

The same town that had shunned him.

He pulled his hand away even though every fiber of his being wanted to say to hell with Austin, to crush her in his arms and never let go.

He concentrated on opening the box.

A navy blue photo album lay inside, nestled in tissue paper. Jesse pulled the album free and turned to the first page to see several landscape shots of Lost Gun. The surrounding trees, the lush pasture, the historic buildings lining Main Street. He flipped through several more pages, saw more pictures of the town, including James Lee and the kids at the car wash and even one of each of his brothers. Billy two-stepped his way around the dance floor down at the local honky-tonk and Cole held tight to an ornery bronc.

"It's a memory book. I know you don't have good memories of your childhood, but these are new memories. Good ones to replace the old ones."

Jesse simply stared and flipped until he reached the last page, which held a full glossy of himself astride one of his training bulls. He swallowed the baseball-size lump in his throat. With stiff fingers he managed to close the book. "It's missing something."

She looked genuinely puzzled. "What?"

His gaze captured hers. "You."

"I don't think this is the right time—"

"Do you love me? Because if you do, I need to hear it."

Fear brightened her eyes, made her hands tremble, and for a split second, he thought she was going to turn and run without ever admitting the truth to him. To herself.

"Yes."

The word sang through his head, echoed through his heart. He wanted to hear her say it again and again, to feel the one syllable against his lips. "Then come with me. You don't have to stay here for your sister. She's all grown up now, living her own life. She doesn't need you here. The town doesn't need you."

"But I need it." Tears filled her voice, betraying the calm she always tried so hard to maintain. "All I could think about for so long was getting out. It's all I dreamed of. I wanted to hit the road, to find someplace where I felt at home. But once I stopped trying to run, I realized that I felt it here. This is home for me, Jesse. It'll always be home."

He stepped toward her and touched his mouth to hers. The photo album thudded to the ground. Jesse wrapped his arms around Gracie and held tight, as if he never meant to let go. He gave her a gentle, searing kiss that intensified the ache deep inside him and made him want to hold her forever.

She loved him, he loved her. This was crazy. They could have a life together starting now. Today. In Austin. Or here.

It didn't matter to him.

The realization hit just as she pulled away.

This was home. Gracie was home.

Her warmth. Her smile. Her love.

It was all right here, and that was why he'd been stalling. This was where he needed to be.

He needed to stay.

And she needed him to go.

Because he knew she would never forgive him if she thought that he'd changed his plans just for her. She would never forgive herself.

Maybe she would. Maybe she'd be happy he'd changed his mind and they'd live happily ever after.

It wasn't a chance he could take. He didn't want her feeling as though she'd destroyed his dreams. Trapped him.

He knew what it felt like to live with guilt. He wouldn't doom her to the hell he'd faced for so long. The doubt. The uncertainty.

"You know where to find me," he murmured against

her soft, sweet lips. "If you change your mind." While he knew with dead certainty that they were meant to be together, Gracie had to discover it for herself.

And if she didn't?

Jesse shoved his greatest fear aside and did the hardest thing he'd ever had to do in his life. He walked away from Gracie Stone.

And then he left Lost Gun for good.

"FORGET THE PICS at the bouncy house!" Trina motioned Gracie toward the large tent set up at the far end of the fairgrounds. It was the first day of the town's infamous three-week-long rodeo and barbecue cook-off, a huge event that drew tourists and fans from all over the state. "Cletus Walker is this close to breaking the record for eating the most bread-and-butter pickles. He's already eaten four hundred and twenty. He'll either blow or land himself in the *Guinness Book of World Records*. Either way, you're going to want firsthand shots."

Gracie clicked off two more shots of three-year-old Sally Wheeler sitting midbounce with her big toe in her mouth and rushed after the town's new mayor.

Rushed. That described her life over the past three weeks since she'd resigned as mayor, handed over the office to the new mayor-elect—Trina—and bought out June Silsbee's photography studio. June was now awaiting the birth of her triplets in peace. Meanwhile, Gracie was up to her armpits in work.

Between babies and youth sports and local chili cook-offs, she barely had time to look through her viewfinder before she was hustling off to the next assignment.

Not that she minded the whirlwind. She welcomed it

because it kept her busy. Too busy to think about Jesse and the all-important fact that she missed him terribly.

"Are you okay?" Trina asked as Gracie caught up to her at the entrance to the pickle-eating tent.

"Fine."

"Uh-huh." Trina gave her a quick once-over. "I'm the mayor, sugar. You can't put anything over on me."

"I think I might be coming down with something."

"Yeah, a bad case of the gimmes."

"What?"

"You know. The gimmes. It's when a woman's been getting some and then all of a sudden she's not getting any. She goes into withdrawal and her body is like, 'Gimme, gimme, gimme.'"

"That's ridiculous."

And all too true.

"I just need a little vitamin C and I'll be fine."

That was what she said, but she wasn't placing any bets. While she'd done the right thing and let him go, a part of her still wished that she had begged him to stay.

Not that it would have made any difference. He would have left anyway. He'd had to leave.

She understood that.

She just wished it didn't hurt so much.

She forced aside the depressing thought, made her way up to the front of the tent and focused on a red-faced Cletus, who eyed pickle number 421 as if it were a snake about to bite him.

She documented the momentous occasion as he devoured the last bite and lifted his arms in victory before making her way toward the corral set up at the far end of the fairgrounds. Dozens of rookie bull riders lined the metal fence, cheering on the wrangler atop the angry bull twisting and turning center stage. The preliminaries hadn't actually started, but the cowboys were giving it their all in a practice round that would pick the lineup for the main event.

She maneuvered between two button-down Western shirts and started snapping pictures.

She aimed for another picture and a strange awareness skittered over her skin, as if someone watched her.

As if…

She glanced around, her gaze searching the dozens of faces.

It was just her imagination, she finally concluded, turning her attention back to her camera. Because no way in heaven, hell or even Texas could Jesse Chisholm be here—

The thought scattered the minute she sighted the familiar face in her viewfinder.

He'd stepped from behind a group of wranglers. The crowd milled around him and the noise rose up, but her full attention fixated on him. She watched as he talked to some cowboy who stood next to him, obviously oblivious to his surroundings, and her hope took a nosedive. For a split second, she thought that he'd come for her, that he was going to sweep her up into his arms and whisk her away.

Right.

He was obviously here for the rodeo. To ride his way straight to another buckle.

Without her.

The thought sent a burst of panic through her because as happy as she was here in Lost Gun, she could never be truly happy without him. She loved him. She always had and she always would, and it was time she owned up to it.

She'd made the last move and ended things with him, and now it was time to make the first move and set things right.

She pushed her way through the crowd, working her way around the corral until she came up behind him. A tap on the shoulder and he turned to face her.

Where she'd expected surprise, she saw only relief. As if he'd been waiting for her for a very long time.

He had, she realized as he stared deep into her eyes and she saw the insecurity, the doubt, the guilt. He'd been waiting for twelve years for her to admit her feelings, to tell the world, and now it was time.

Her gaze snagged on the weariness in his eyes and her heart hitched. "You look like hell," she said as she noted the tight lines around his mouth, the shadows beneath his eyes, as if he hadn't slept in days. Weeks.

"Nice to see you, too."

"You here to compete?"

"That, and I thought you might want these back." Two fingers wiggled into his jeans pocket and he pulled a familiar scrap of black lace from inside. He grinned his infamous rodeo-bad-boy grin that made her insides jump as he dangled her undies from one tanned finger. "These do belong to you, don't they?"

A few weeks ago she would have snatched the undies from his hand and stuffed them in her purse, desperate to keep up appearances and avoid any scandal that would disappoint the good folks of Lost Gun. But things were different now. She was different. She loved Jesse and she didn't care who knew it. She gave in to the smile that tugged at her lips. "They are, but I don't see that I need them at the moment. I'm wearing new ones."

"I know. I thought maybe we could make a trade."

"So you're collecting women's lingerie?"

"Just yours, Gracie. Only yours. I was hoping to add every damn pair you possess to my stash." Determination lit his eyes. "Just so you know, I might have retreated, but I'm not giving up. I would never try to force you to do anything. I've been staying away to let you know that I respect your decisions, and I'll keep staying away if I have to. If that's what you want." His fingertips trailed along her cheek as if he couldn't quite believe she was real. "Because you're what I want and I don't care who knows it."

"What about Austin? It's your home."

"You're home." His hands cradled her face, his thumbs smoothing across her trembling bottom lip. "Wherever you are, that's where I'll hang my hat."

"You hate it here."

He glanced around at the multitude of faces surrounding them. "I hate my past and the people who refuse to let me forget it. But not everyone here is like that. Miss Hazel is the sweetest woman who ever walked the planet, and she's here." He shrugged. "This place isn't so bad."

"But Austin is your dream. I can't ask you to give up your dream. I won't ask it."

Anger flared deep in his eyes as his mouth tightened into a grim line. "So you don't love me. Is that what you're trying to say?"

"No! I do love you. With all my heart. It's just…I don't want you making all the sacrifices." She shook her head and turned to stare at the bull kicking up dust in a nearby chute. "That's not what love is all about. It's about give-and-take. An equal amount of both."

"Meaning?" He came up behind her, so close she could feel the heat from his body, hear his heart beating in her ears.

"I'm pretty good with this camera," she told him. "I was thinking I could take some time off and follow you out onto the road. If you could use a good action photographer, that is." Her gaze met his. "I do want to live here, but I know you have a job that you love, one that takes you away for weeks on end. I don't want to be away from you that long." She caught his arms when he started to reach for her and held him off, determined to resolve the unanswered questions between them. "I'm willing to follow you—I want to follow you—if you're willing to follow me right back here when it's all said and done. Give-and-take. Fifty-fifty. You and me."

"What about your sister?"

"She's a big girl. She doesn't need me."

"I'd be willing to bet she still needs you."

She shrugged. "True, but I'm just a text away. So that's it. That's my offer. You let me go with you and I'll let you come back here with me."

He grinned, the sight easing the anxiety that had been coiling inside her. "I could use a new head shot or two," he declared as he drew her into his arms and hugged her fiercely. "To keep the fans happy."

"Not too happy," she said, her heart swelling with the certainty that he loved her as much as she loved him. "I don't share very well."

"Neither do I." His expression went from sheer happiness to serious desperation. "Marry me, Gracie, and we'll make a home for ourselves right here in Lost Gun.

You can take pictures to your heart's content and do anything that makes you happy, as long as we're together. I want you in my bed." He touched one nipple and brought the tip to throbbing awareness. "In my heart." His hand slid higher, over the pounding between her breasts. "In my life." His thumb came to rest over the frantic jump of her pulse. "Everywhere."

She smiled through a blurry haze of tears and pulled away from him to grab the hem of her sundress and run her hands up her bare legs.

His expression went from puzzled to hungry. "What are you doing?"

She smiled wider. "Giving you a deposit."

She shimmied and wiggled until her hot pink panties pooled at her ankles. Stepping free, she dangled the scrap of silk in front of him before stuffing the undies into his pocket along with the other pair already in his possession.

"Just so you know, there's more where those came from. A future of them. Forever." And then she kissed him, surrendering her body to his roaming hands, her heart to his and her soul to whatever the future held.

Right here in Lost Gun.

Epilogue

"YOU SURE YOU WANT to do this?" Jesse asked Gracie as he braked to a stop near the fence that surrounded Big Earl Jessup's property. He killed the engine on the pickup and flicked off the headlights.

"No." Gracie tamped down on her anxiety when she heard the dogs start to bark and held tight to the hand of the man sitting next to her. "But Jackie Sue Patterson told Martin Skolnik who told Laura Lynn McKinney who just so happened to mention when she brought her twins into the studio for pics that she saw Casey Jessup at the hardware store yesterday. She bought two propane lanterns, some rope, a tarp and some tie-down stakes. That means she's cooking moonshine again and I'm the one responsible since I let her off with just a warning instead of turning her over to Sheriff Hooker."

He squeezed her hand reassuringly. "It could just mean she's going camping."

"Maybe, but maybe not. Either way, I need to find out. If something's up, we'll head back to town and I'll notify the sheriff." For Casey's own good.

While Gracie knew the girl was just helping out

her grandfather the only way she knew how, cooking moonshine was still illegal. And dangerous. And Gracie wouldn't be able to live with herself if something bad happened and someone got hurt.

She eyed the small house that sat several yards away. A television flickered just beyond one of the windows, but otherwise everything seemed quiet.

She whipped out her binoculars and scoured the area, from the old toilet that had been turned into a planter near the front porch, to the stretch of pasture that extended beyond the house. Her heart stalled when she noted the small light that flickered in the far distance.

"See?" She pointed and handed Jesse the binoculars. "It's her."

"It's definitely someone." He gazed at the horizon before handing the binoculars back to her. "I don't know that it's Casey."

"Who else would it be?" Gracie watched as the figure lifted the pinpoint of light and suddenly Casey Jessup's face came into view. "It's her." The young woman turned and walked toward the tree line, lantern in one hand and what looked like a shovel in the other. "I told you she was up to something."

"She's walking."

"Exactly."

"And carrying a light."

"Even more incriminating."

"Babe, she could just be going for a walk."

"At half past midnight?"

"Maybe she's meeting someone."

"To sell a few cases."

"Or to hook up." He shrugged. "It *is* one hell of a nice night."

She abandoned the binoculars to slide him a glance. Her heart hitched as her gaze collided with his and she felt the familiar warmth that told her she was sitting next to her soul mate. A man who loved her as much as she loved him. A man who always would.

She noted the gleam in his rich, violet eyes. "Since when did you turn into the eternal optimist?"

A grin tugged at his lips. "Since a certain buttoned-up city official whipped off her panties in the middle of town and handed them to me in front of God and the Amberjack twins."

Her own lips twitched at the memory. "I did give them something to talk about, didn't I?"

"Enough fuel to keep things interesting for at least another year." He winked. "It was definitely one of my most favorite moments."

"Glad I could renew your hope in mankind."

"Sugar, you *are* my hope." He leaned across the seat and touched her lips with his own in a fierce kiss that made her stomach quiver.

It had been a week since she'd handed her panties to him in front of an arena full of people and declared her love. A busy week since Jesse had changed his mind about selling his dad's old place and decided to clear the spot and build a brand-new house smack-dab in the middle of Lost Gun.

Not that he'd made complete peace with his past.

We're talking a week.

The recent airing of *Famous Texas Outlaws* had, as expected, lured a ton of tourists to town and stirred a wave of fortune hunting. And speculation. About the money. About Jesse and his brothers and their integrity. According to the latest round of gossip, they not only knew what had happened to the money, but they'd gone on a spending spree that included everything from new cowboy boots to a private island in South America.

Crazy, but that was the rumor mill in a small town. And part of the reason Jesse had been so desperate to get out of Lost Gun for good.

But while he'd yet to forgive the townspeople who'd made his life a living hell while growing up—the same people who were wagging their tongues and feeding the frenzy right now—he had managed to acknowledge those people who did accept him. Even more, he'd found the strength to forgive himself.

And so even though it had only been a week, the past didn't hurt quite so much. And when it eventually did, Gracie would be right there to soothe the ache.

She loved him and he loved her and they were now focused on the future. Lost Gun's infamous three-week-long rodeo extravaganza was in full swing. Jesse had swept the preliminaries and landed at the top of the leader board. Meanwhile Gracie had been named the official photographer by the board of directors of the Lost Gun Livestock Show and Rodeo. Her pictures had been featured on the front page of the weekly newspaper just yesterday and her photography studio was booked solid for the weeks to come.

Speaking of which, she had an early shoot tomorrow morning and the last thing she needed was to be traipsing around in the middle of the night.

At the same time, she would never forgive herself if something bad happened to Casey or Big Earl.

While she'd given up carrying the weight of the world, old habits were still hard to break.

Before she could pull back and tell Jesse as much, he ended the kiss, pulled his keys from the ignition and reached for the door. "Let's get this over with so that we can get on with our own hookup."

"Such a romantic."

"It will be, darlin'." He winked. "That much I can guarantee."

She tamped down the excitement the blatant promise stirred in her and reached for the door handle. A few minutes and a full stretch of pasture later, they reached a cluster of trees. They picked their way through the thick foliage, following the small light that glowed in the distance until they reached the line of trees that gave way to yet another pasture. The light grew brighter, illuminating Casey Jessup and the shovel in her hands.

Gracie watched as the young woman shoved the sharp edge into the ground, pushed it down with her foot and scooped a mound of dirt to the side.

"That doesn't look like a still to me," Jesse whispered against her ear.

"Maybe she's burying the evidence. People bury everything from money to time capsules. Why not moonshine?"

"Because the goal is to sell it, not bury it," he pointed out under his breath. "Something else is up."

He was right, Gracie realized as she watched Casey dig not one, but two holes. Then three. Four.

Forget burying something. The woman was looking. Desperately looking, her movements frantic, anxious, determined.

She finished another hole and let loose a loud cuss as she hit another dead end.

Still, she didn't give up. She went for yet another spot, her expression mad. *Mean.*

The minute the thought struck, something niggled at Gracie's subconscious. Her mind rifled back and she remembered the meeting with Big Earl and the Josey Wales poster on the wall. The quote echoed in her head, so familiar, as if she'd heard it somewhere before.

She had, she realized as she held Jesse's hand and watched Casey Jessup break ground at another spot.

When things look bad and it looks like you're not gonna make it, then you gotta get mean. I mean plumb, mad-dog mean. 'Cause if you lose your head and you give up then you neither live nor win.

It was the quote engraved on Silas Chisholm's headstone. It had been his favorite saying or so Jesse had told her when they'd visited his grave just a few short days ago.

He'd been a die-hard Josey Wales fan, just like Big Earl.

"They knew each other," she murmured, the words louder than she intended.

Casey's head snapped up and she turned. Her gaze locked with Gracie's and a dozen emotions rolled across her face. Surprise. Aggravation. Relief.

"He knew Silas, didn't he?" The words were out before Gracie could stop them.

Casey didn't look as if she meant to answer.

No, she looked ready to come at them, shovel swinging. But the anger quickly subsided as her gaze shifted to Jesse and something close to defeat filled her expression. She shook her head. "He didn't just know him. They were friends. Partners." She slung the shovel down and stuck a hand on her hip. "You said we couldn't cook anymore and we need that money." Her gaze met Gracie's. "I can't take care of Big Earl like I need to. He's got heart problems and he needs that money."

"What money?" Gracie asked, but she already knew.

And so did Jesse. "It wasn't lost in the fire," Jesse murmured after a long, drawn-out moment. "It's here."

Casey nodded. "Silas gave it to Great-granddaddy and he buried it out here for safekeeping."

"That's great." Gracie's heart pumped with the realization of what such a discovery meant. Recovering the money would put an end to the treasure hunting and the speculation. The money would mean real closure.

For the town, and for Jesse.

"Actually, it's not so great." Casey blew out a deep, exasperated breath and stared around her at the multitude of holes. "Great-granddaddy's memory isn't what it used to be. He buried the money out here, but the thing is, he can't remember exactly where." She glanced behind her at the endless expanse of land that seemed to stretch endlessly. "We've got fifty acres and the only thing he can remember for sure is that he buried it in some tall grass."

Gracie stared around, at the endless stretch of tall grass and trees and enough possibilities to keep Casey Jessup digging night after night for the rest of eternity.

"It could be anywhere," Jesse's deep voice echoed in the dark night, confirming what Gracie was already thinking.

That there would be no quick fix. No digging it up

and giving it back, and laying the past to rest for Jesse and his brothers.

Not just yet, that is.

* * * * *

Be sure to look for Kimberly Raye's next book in her trilogy about the sexy Chisholm brothers—
TEXAS OUTLAWS: BILLY!
Available from Harlequin Blaze in February 2014.

#783 A SEAL's SALVATION
Uniformly Hot!
by Tawny Weber
Good girl Genna Reilly saved Brody Lane once when her attempted seduction got him shanghaied into the Navy. Can her love save this sexy SEAL again, now that his world is falling apart?

#784 TEXAS OUTLAWS: BILLY
The Texas Outlaws
by Kimberly Raye
Rodeo cowboy Billy Chisholm wants one hot night of wild, unforgettable sex. Unfortunately, he gets more than he bargains for when he meets Sabrina Collins, who not only gets into his head, but finds a place in his heart.

#785 GAME ON
Last Bachelor Standing
by Nancy Warren
Adam Shawnigan is sexy, single...and in serious trouble when performance coach Serena Long is hired to improve his hockey skills. Now there's another game in play—and Adam's bachelorhood is in jeopardy!

#786 HARD TO HOLD
The U.S. Marshals
by Karen Foley
Reformed con artist Maddie Howe must revert to her former ways in order to rescue her brother, even if it means kidnapping the hunky U.S. marshal who is hot on her trail!

REQUEST YOUR FREE BOOKS!
2 FREE NOVELS PLUS 2 FREE GIFTS!

HARLEQUIN

Blaze®

red-hot reads!

YES! Please send me 2 FREE Harlequin® Blaze™ novels and my 2 FREE gifts (gifts are worth about $10). After receiving them, if I don't wish to receive any more books, I can return the shipping statement marked "cancel." If I don't cancel, I will receive 4 brand-new novels every month and be billed just $4.74 per book in the U.S. or $4.96 per book in Canada. That's a savings of at least 14% off the cover price. It's quite a bargain. Shipping and handling is just 50¢ per book in the U.S. and 75¢ per book in Canada.* I understand that accepting the 2 free books and gifts places me under no obligation to buy anything. I can always return a shipment and cancel at any time. Even if I never buy another book, the two free books and gifts are mine to keep forever.

150/350 HDN F4WC

Name _____ (PLEASE PRINT) _____

Address _____ Apt. #

City _____ State/Prov. _____ Zip/Postal Code

Signature (if under 18, a parent or guardian must sign)

Mail to the **Harlequin® Reader Service:**
IN U.S.A.: P.O. Box 1867, Buffalo, NY 14240-1867
IN CANADA: P.O. Box 609, Fort Erie, Ontario L2A 5X3

Want to try two free books from another line?
Call 1-800-873-8635 or visit www.ReaderService.com.

* Terms and prices subject to change without notice. Prices do not include applicable taxes. Sales tax applicable in N.Y. Canadian residents will be charged applicable taxes. Offer not valid in Quebec. This offer is limited to one order per household. Not valid for current subscribers to Harlequin Blaze books. All orders subject to credit approval. Credit or debit balances in a customer's account(s) may be offset by any other outstanding balance owed by or to the customer. Please allow 4 to 6 weeks for delivery. Offer available while quantities last.

Your Privacy—The Harlequin® Reader Service is committed to protecting your privacy. Our Privacy Policy is available online at www.ReaderService.com or upon request from the Harlequin Reader Service.

We make a portion of our mailing list available to reputable third parties that offer products we believe may interest you. If you prefer that we not exchange your name with third parties, or if you wish to clarify or modify your communication preferences, please visit us at www.ReaderService.com/consumerschoice or write to us at Harlequin Reader Service Preference Service, P.O. Box 9062, Buffalo, NY 14269. Include your complete name and address.

HBI3R2

Here's a sneak peek at

A SEAL's Salvation

by Tawny Weber

It all began ten years ago....

"Genna, you're crazy. You don't have to do this."

"Of course I do. You dared me." Genna Reilly gave her best friend a wide-eyed look.

She needed to do this. Now, while anticipation was still zinging through her system, making her feel brave enough to take on the world. Or, in this case, to take down the sexiest bad boy of Bedford, California.

She wanted Brody Lane.

But he had practically made a career of ignoring her existence.

Time to end that.

So tonight, thanks to Dina's dare, she was going to do something about it.

"I don't kiss and tell," Genna murmured.

"You mean you don't kiss or do anything else," Dina corrected, rolling her eyes.

"The dare was to kiss Brody Lane," Sylvie pointed out, glancing nervously toward the garage. "Genna's not going in there unless she follows through."

Genna looked toward the garage, the silhouette of a man working on a motorcycle.

"If I'm not back in ten minutes, head home," she instructed, fluffing her hair and hurrying off.

Carefully she peeked around the open doorway.

There he was. Brody Lane, in all his bare-chested glory. Black hair fell across his eyes as he bent over the Harley. She had the perfect view of his sexy denim-clad butt.

Genna fanned herself. Oh, baby, he was so hot.

She took a deep breath, then stepped through the doorway.

And waited.

Nothing.

"Hey, Brody," she called out, her voice shaking slightly. "How're you doing?"

His body went still, his head turned. His eyes, golden-brown like a cat's, narrowed.

Slowly, he straightened away from the bike, the light glinting off that sleek golden skin. Her gaze traveled from the broad stretch of his shoulders down his tapered waist to his jeans, slung low and loose on his hips.

Oh, wow.

"Genna?" He cast a glance behind her, then back with an arched brow. "What the hell do you want?"

**Pick up A SEAL'S SALVATION
by Tawny Weber, available wherever you buy
Harlequin® Blaze® books.**

She's got game!

Adam Shawnigan is sexy, single...and in serious trouble when performance coach Serena Long is hired to improve his hockey skills. Now there's another game in play—and Adam's bachelorhood is in jeopardy!

Pick up
Game On
by *Nancy Warren,*
available this February wherever you buy Harlequin Blaze books.

Red-Hot Reads
www.Harlequin.com

The stakes are high!

Reformed con artist Maddie Howe must revert to her former ways in order to rescue her brother, even if it means kidnapping the hunky U.S. marshal who is hot on her trail! From the Sierra Nevada foothills to the glittering casinos of Reno, Colton Black will go along as her "hostage" in order to keep her safe, even at the risk of losing his badge—and his heart.

Don't miss
Hard to Hold
by *Karen Foley,*
available this February wherever you buy Harlequin Blaze books.

Red-Hot Reads
www.Harlequin.com

HB79790